"You're Not At All My Type,"

Angela said as her thumb traced the line of his upper lip.

"No," Bryce agreed. "Nor are you mine."

His hand sank into her hair at the nape, holding her head immobilized, and he leaned toward her until his face was only inches from hers. "I'd have to be crazy to get involved with you. But I'm tired of being sensible," he growled. "Tonight I don't want to be careful. I want to take you to bed. To feel your body under mine."

Angela shivered. "What if I said yes?"

Award-winning author Kristin James "touches readers' hearts."

—*Romantic Times*

Dear Reader,

Welcome to the wonderful world of Silhouette Desire! This month, look for six scintillating love stories. I know you're going to enjoy them all. First up is *The Beauty, the Beast and the Baby*, a fabulous MAN OF THE MONTH from Dixie Browning. It's also the second book in her TALL, DARK AND HANDSOME miniseries.

The exciting SONS AND LOVERS series also continues with Leanne Banks's *Ridge: The Avenger*. This is Leanne's first Silhouette Desire, but she certainly isn't new to writing romance.

This month, Desire has *Husband: Optional,* the next installment of Marie Ferrarella's THE BABY OF THE MONTH CLUB. Don't worry if you've missed earlier titles in this series, because this book "stands alone." And it's so charming and breezy you're sure to just love it!

The WEDDING BELLES series by Carole Buck is completed with *Zoe and the Best Man*. This series just keeps getting better and better, and Gabriel Flynn is one scrumptious hero.

Next is Kristin James' Desire, *The Last Groom on Earth*, a delicious opposites-attract story written with Kristin's trademark sensuality.

Rounding out the month is an amnesia story (one of my *favorite* story twists), *Just a Memory Away,* by award-winning author Helen R. Myers.

And *next* month, we're beginning CELEBRATION 1000, a very exciting, ultraspecial three-month promotion celebrating the publication of the 1000th Silhouette Desire. During April, May and June, look for books by some of your most beloved writers, including Mary Lynn Baxter, Annette Broadrick, Joan Johnston, Cait London, Ann Major and Diana Palmer, who is actually writing book #1000! These will be months to remember, filled with "keepers."

As always, I wish you the very best,

Lucia Macro
Senior Editor

KRISTIN JAMES
THE LAST GROOM ON EARTH

SILHOUETTE *Desire*

™ Published by Silhouette Books
America's Publisher of Contemporary Romance

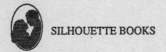 SILHOUETTE BOOKS

ISBN 0-373-05986-8

THE LAST GROOM ON EARTH

Printed in U.S.A.

KRISTIN JAMES

is a former attorney married to a family counselor, and
they have a young daughter. Her family and her writing keep her busy, but when she does have free time,
she loves to read. In addition to her contemporary
romances, she has written a number of historicals.

One

___

Bryce Richards had thought he was ready for anything when it came to Angela Hewitt, but he found that he was wrong. He was not prepared to walk into the offices of H & A Enterprises and find a witch standing on a stool in the middle of the room.

He stopped, struck dumb, and simply gaped at the woman on the stool. Another woman knelt at her feet, mumbling something as she fingered the hem of the witch's dress. Bryce wondered for one mad moment if he had stumbled into some sort of pagan ceremony. Then the kneeling woman let out a yelp of pain and reached up to remove the pins she held clenched between her teeth.

"Would you stop wriggling?" she asked irritably. "I'll never get this hem fixed at this rate."

Bryce realized with relief that the woman on the floor was measuring a hem on the "witch's" dress. He

looked more closely at what the "witch" wore. It was
long and flowing and black, clinging tightly to her
torso, then floating out loosely below her hips in lay-
ers of some diaphanous material. The edges of each
layer were cut in a zigzag fashion so that it hung in
points, and the ends of the loose sleeves were cut in the
same way. It was this cut and the color of the dress
that had made him think immediately of a witch's
costume. Now, looking at the plunging V-cut neckline of the dress, he realized that it must be some sort
of odd evening gown. It was, he told himself, much
too sexy for riding broomsticks and casting spells.

His eyes lingered on the neckline. The woman's
breasts were full and creamy white, pushing up and
out of the black material in a way that made his fingers itch to curve over the lush flesh. He dropped his
gaze lower, moving over the material that clung to her
breasts, waist and hips as if it were a second skin. His
loins tightened in response. *Who was this woman, and
what on earth was she doing dressed like this and
standing in the middle of a business office?*

Then he looked up, and he knew. It was Angela
Hewitt herself. He could not see her face; her head was
bent as she peered down at the woman working on her
hem. But that shock of curling red hair could belong
to only one person. He remembered it clearly, even if
it had been almost fourteen years—and even if it now
hung in burnished, inviting curls instead of braids or
a wild tangle. He should have known, Bryce thought.
Trust Angela Hewitt to be under investigation by the
IRS and yet be unconcernedly trying on evening gowns
in the middle of her office.

Angela glanced up at him, then turned and called
out, "Hey, somebody's appointment is here!"

Bryce glanced around the room for the first time. It was large, the wide main hall of the old house near downtown Raleigh in which H & A Enterprises was located. A receptionist's desk, vacant at the moment, stood to one side of the elegant curved staircase. The rest of the hallway was empty, sweeping back in a dazzling expanse of gleaming gold oak flooring to a swinging door at the opposite end. On either side of the hallway, several doors stood open. A few heads popped out of the doors at Angela's announcement, and the swinging door in the back opened, and a man peered out.

Everyone looked at Bryce blankly. Then they turned to look at Angela.

"Hey, Angie, looking good," one of the young men commented, and another let out a wolf whistle.

Angela grimaced at the man who had whistled. "I don't know. Somehow, I don't think Maladora is really me. I mean, whoever heard of an evil sorceress with freckles and red hair?"

One of the women watching chuckled and said, "Then why don't you go as Princess Alicia?"

Bryce's cool gray gaze swept over the scene. This hardly looked like a well-run business, with the employees hanging in their doorways, the owner creating a distraction in the middle of the office, and all of them sounding like the inhabitants of a madhouse. He suspected that their accounting procedures were just as lax. *No wonder the IRS was breathing down their necks.*

"Nah, I was her last year," Angela answered offhandedly. "I was a medieval lady the year before. And I think a Southern belle is way too overdone."

She turned to Bryce and asked seriously, "What do you think? Do I look like Maladora to you?"

"I don't know," Bryce responded crisply, "since I have no idea what or who Maladora is. Miss Hewitt, if I could speak with you..."

Angela looked at him, slightly puzzled, then her eyes narrowed. "You!" She spat out the word in recognition. "You're Bryce Richards!" From the tone of her voice, she might have been saying, "Jack the Ripper!"

"Yes." He nodded his head in greeting.

"What are you doing here?" Angela frowned at him darkly.

"Your parents asked me to—"

"*Arrgh.*" Angela made an exasperated noise deep in her throat and, holding up her skirts, lithely hopped off the stool. "I might have known they'd do something like this," she announced to no one in particular, then turned, with an eloquent swish of her skirts, and stalked toward the stairs.

Bryce followed her. She whirled at the foot of the stairs and glared at him. "Go away. I don't need you. Nor do I need my parents sending their flunky down here to pester me."

"I can see that you still have the same charming personality," Bryce began, then stopped. He reminded himself that he intended to hold onto his temper. He was determined not to let Angela get to him, as she had done so many times years ago.

"And I can see that *you* are still the same prig you always were," she snapped back. She drew a breath to say more, but then she glanced up at the top of the stairs, where several more interested spectators had gathered, and she shut her mouth with a snap.

Angela cast him a withering glance—just as if, Bryce thought with a growing sense of indignation, it had been *he* who was creating this scene. Then she turned and stomped up the stairs and into the room at the top, closing her door behind her with a loud crack.

Angela was furious. She reached back, unzipped her dress and ripped it off, wadding it into a ball and hurling it at a chair in the corner of the room. She might have known, she thought. *Trust her parents to decide that she was too incompetent to handle this problem and then send down their Boy Scout to tell her what to do.*

Damn Bryce Richards! She hadn't even thought about him for years. Now he showed up, and all the old feelings of inadequacy, resentment and rejection came flooding in on her.

Angela set her jaw as she stalked over to her desk and jerked on the jeans and T-shirt that she had been wearing before she tried on the costume. She remembered that first day when she had come into the den of her family home in Charlotte and found Bryce sitting with her mother, discussing some horribly boring math problem that Angela hadn't even understood, and her mother had been beaming at him like a proud parent with a precocious child. Angela's heart had immediately dropped down to her socks.

All her life she had never fit in with her family. Her mother was a professor of accounting of some note, and her father was a banker. Both sides of the family were littered with hardheaded businessmen, engineers, actuaries and scientists. All of them were levelheaded, logical, systematic people whose every decision was based on a rational analysis of the options.

Angela's sister, Jenny, had fit in with them; Angela could remember her actually becoming excited when she figured out the key to a difficult math assignment. Grown now, she worked in the bank and had married a chemical engineer.

Angela, on the other hand, had been flighty, daydreaming and impulsive. Her decisions were made on an instinctive, gut-level feeling, and she found math courses boring. Her favorite subject was literature, and she preferred to spend her days hidden in some nook or other, reading about knights and fair maidens, adventure and romance. She remembered once, when she had been sitting in front of the television, enthralled in an old black-and-white swashbuckler, her science homework open and forgotten on her lap, her mother had come into the room and found her. Marina Hewitt had said nothing, simply stared at her daughter in dismay and astonishment. Angela had felt like crying. It wasn't simply that her mother disapproved of her neglecting her homework to watch an old movie. What was more upsetting to Angela was that Marina could not comprehend why anyone would even want to do such a thing.

Angela had never felt quite a part of her family. By the age of twelve, when Bryce Richards came on the scene, she was convinced that everything about her was wrong. Though she had wanted and tried all her life to fit in with the other Hewitts, she had never been able to, and the attempt to do so had made her miserable. The years of intensive math courses ahead of her, which her parents had planned on, seemed like sheer punishment. She didn't want to be methodical;

she didn't want to plan out her high school, her college and then her life. She wanted to be free and easy, to go where the winds of fortune took her. Yet at the same time, she felt guilty for rebelling against her parents, for not wanting to be another model daughter, and she could not squelch the old desire that her parents love her just as she was.

Then Bryce, Mr. Perfect, had come along. He was one of her mother's students in a night course she taught at the local university, and Marina had taken him on as her protégé. He had come over to visit frequently. Her parents invited him to dinner, sometimes took him with them on family outings, spent long hours talking to him. He shared her parents' interests. He admired and respected them. Or, as the twelve-year-old Angela had seen it, he spent most of his time buttering them up. In Angela's opinion, he was a gawky, thin boy of nineteen, a dopey numbers nerd—the epitome of everything she disliked. Worse than that, it was obvious to her that her parents adored him, which only confirmed what kind of feeling they must have for her, his opposite. Her parents were taking him in, a sort of surrogate son, and as a consequence she would be, she knew, squeezed even further out of the family.

In short, in Bryce Richards she had seen her enemy. The battleground was her house, and her parents, the prize. She played childish tricks on him at every opportunity, and the scoldings and groundings she received from her parents for those tricks only made her dislike Bryce more. The harder she tried to defeat him, the more she was separated from her family. Finally, after a year, she had given up. She admitted to herself that he had won, and she had lost.

She withdrew into her own interests, spending hours curled up in her room reading science fiction and fantasy or zapping enemies with her joystick in front of the game console and TV set. When Bryce was around, she made it a point to stay out of sight. By the time she was fifteen, Bryce had graduated from college and gone to another city to work. He and her parents had always stayed in touch, but Angela had never inquired about him. She had not seen him again until today.

She groaned and buried her head in her hands, leaning her elbows against the desk. *What a time for him to pop up again!* It was the last straw to have to put up with him when she was already under the stress of a threatened IRS investigation—and with her latest project only half done and her deadline a few more weeks away. What made it even more awful was the fact that her parents had told Bryce about her problems, had asked him to come rushing down here and save her—indeed, she was sure that they must have *begged* him, in order to get him to help her.

She had enjoyed a better relationship with her parents the past few years. They hadn't been able to argue with the obvious success of her business; all the silly impulsive things she had done, which they had moaned over, had turned out to be highly profitable in the long run. And with the miles between Raleigh and Charlotte to separate them, she and her parents had achieved a certain friendliness, almost adult to adult.

That they had turned around and spilled all her troubles to Bryce Richards was a betrayal of that newly achieved closeness. *And they had asked him to come save her, too!—as if she were a baby, an incom-*

petent. It was humiliating. Bryce was the last, the *last* person she wanted helping her. Not only did he probably share her parents' assessment of her as a scatterbrained nincompoop, but she also felt sure that he thoroughly disliked her, as well. After all, she had been mean to him as only a hurt twelve-year-old can be, and she doubted whether he had forgotten. He had a memory like an elephant's—worse, like an accountant's.

There was a loud rap on the door, and a fraction of a second later, it opened, framing Bryce Richards in the doorway. He was frowning, his mouth tightly compressed, and his face looked carved out of stone. He was certainly no longer the gawky young man she remembered, Angela thought to herself. It was no wonder that it had taken her a few moments to recognize him. He was tall, of course, but his body was rock-solid now, and he moved with confidence and surety. She had not remembered him as being so handsome, and she wondered if it was maturity that had changed his face or if she had simply been too blinded by her dislike of him to notice the clean-cut lines of his face. His eyes had always been intense, but fifteen years ago, she had not realized how attractive their odd silvery gray color was.

"What are you doing following me?" Angela snapped, irritated at the foolish way her thoughts were wandering. Even as she said it, she realized how childishly petty she sounded. She blushed, embarrassed and even more irritated that she could so easily fall back into long-ago patterns.

"I drove all the way down here from Charlotte because Marina asked me to. I'm not going to turn around and drive back just because you're too pig-headed—"

"Well, you could have saved yourself the trouble of the trip," Angela retorted, "if you had bothered to call me first. I would have told you that I don't need your help."

His eyebrows rose in a sardonic expression of disbelief, and he moved forward into the room. He sat down in the chair in front of her desk and folded his hands, looking at her with a galling air of patience, as if she were a child or mentally defective.

"You don't need help when the IRS has your company under investigation?"

"Mother had no right to tell you about it."

Bryce shrugged. "She was concerned about you."

Angela wanted to snap back that Marina was concerned because she thought that Angela couldn't do anything, but she kept her lips shut tight against the words. Both she and Bryce might know that that was her mother's opinion, but she wasn't about to admit it to him.

"We'll manage just fine without your help."

"Wait a minute," a voice said from the doorway.

Angela looked up to see a short, slightly balding man with a round face and a warm smile standing outside the doorway, peering in interestedly. Angela groaned inwardly.

"Who is this guy? What's he talking about?" the man went on.

"Yeah." A blond woman who had been standing just to the side of the door stuck her head inside, also. "I'm not sure we want to turn down help quite so quickly."

Angela sighed. "Hello, Kelly. Tim. Can't a person have a private conversation around here?"

Kelly cocked her head, looking judicious, then said, "It's hard. Particularly when your door's open."

"And you started your argument downstairs in front of everyone," Tim added.

"All right. Tim, Kelly, this is Bryce Richards. He's a friend of my parents. Bryce, this is Timothy Allen, my partner, and Kelly Beeckman, our chief financial officer."

Kelly grinned and amended, "Head bookkeeper, in other words."

Tim smiled at Bryce and reached out to shake his hand. "Nice to meet you. You've known Angela a long time?"

"Since I was twelve," Angela said shortly. "I was just telling Bryce that we can handle the IRS problem. We have the C.P.A. who did our taxes, and we hired a tax attorney."

"And with their help, you've gone from an ordinary audit into a full-blown investigation." Bryce pointed this out casually.

Angela shot him a fulminating glance. Tim's round face grew worried, and Kelly began to chew at her lower lip.

"Look, Angela, if Mr. Richards thinks he can help..." Kelly began.

"My parents are interfering, that's all."

Tim ignored her and turned toward Bryce. "What makes Mr. and Mrs. Hewitt think you can help us?"

"Because I'm an auditor. I've worked for the IRS and as an auditor for the Feds. Now I have my own company in Charlotte, and our specialty is fiscal investigation."

"Fiscal investigation?" Tim looked blank. "What's that mean?"

"Well, basically, it's that we find errors and fraud. We're sort of a security company in the financial arena. We study corporate systems of accounting and set up ways to avoid theft and fraud. We find leaks and duplications of work. We outline plans to trim the fat."

Tim's eyes widened. "Why, that sounds like you could help us." He turned to look inquiringly at Angela.

"We don't need him." Angela crossed her arms defensively. "Besides, it'll cost a fortune, and we're already paying for that expensive tax attorney—and the whole reason the IRS is suspicious is because they think we aren't making enough money! How can we afford to hire him?"

"I'm not charging you." Bryce interrupted quietly. "I'm doing this as a favor to your mother."

"Oh." Somehow Angela felt even more irritated by this fact. "I'm not a charity case," she told him coldly. "If we need your services, we'll pay for them."

"Of course. It isn't as if we haven't made any money the past few years," Tim said jovially. "We just had higher expenses the last year—more staff, more development costs, that sort of thing. But we're still strong. We're making good money. Angela's just upset."

Angela made a strangled noise in her throat, and Tim glanced over at her. "Well, it's true, Angie. Everyone is. How could we not be with the government sniffing around like we're some kind of criminals? I think we ought to let Mr. Richards try, see what he can come up with."

"I don't know..." Kelly said doubtfully, looking at Angela, then back at Tim. "If there's something wrong, we would have found it already. Maybe the IRS is on a wild-goose chase. They haven't told us what they expect to find, have they?"

"No. They've been frustratingly tight-lipped." Angela was pleased that Kelly was supporting her. "They're just poking into our records and making a nuisance of themselves. I don't think they even know what they're looking for."

"Maybe they don't," Bryce agreed. "But if you think that the IRS is going to look at a few records, then shrug their shoulders and leave, you're incredibly naive. Once they're on your trail, they'll be after you till they get you."

"But there's nothing to get!" Angela burst out. "We've paid our taxes every year. We reported all our income. Our deductions are legal."

"That's true." Tim nodded. "I mean, everything we've done is aboveboard, so we really shouldn't have anything to worry about. It's a nuisance, but in the end they're bound to find out that there's no basis for their suspicions, and they'll drop the investigation."

Bryce turned his cool gray eyes on him for a moment, then began to shake his head. "I think all three of you are in for a rude awakening. The IRS is like a terrier with a rat. Sticking your head in the sand is not going to make them go away."

He paused for a moment. All three of the others in the office stared back at him. Finally he shrugged and stood up. "All right. I can't beat you over the head to make you do it. It's your business." He turned and looked directly at Angela. "I'll tell your mother you prefer to go it on your own. Goodbye, Angela." He nodded at them all. "Good luck."

He didn't need to add the next line. "You'll need it." His expression as he turned away from them made that opinion clear.

He closed the door behind him. Angela leaned back in her chair with a sigh and closed her eyes. "The past few months," she said softly, "have been the worst of my life."

The IRS had begun an audit of their company in January. At first it had seemed perfectly ordinary, and Angela had not been worried, as she was sure that their record-keeping would bear them out. But as the thing went on, it had seemed to mushroom, until Angela had begun to be afraid—so much so that she had divulged her worries to her mother last week on the telephone.

"Amen," Kelly agreed, plopping down in the chair Bryce had just vacated.

Tim began to rub his chin in a familiar nervous habit. "Come on, you guys, cheer up. It'll turn out okay. It has to."

"No, it doesn't." Angela opened her eyes and looked at him. Tim was a sweet guy and a good friend, not to mention an absolute whiz at computers, but he was not a person who liked to face reality. He was more likely to deny an unwelcome truth and ignore it than to try to change it or adapt to it. "What if Bryce is right? What if we are being ostriches? We could lose our whole business."

"Don't say that!" Kelly squeaked.

Angela looked over at the blonde. They had been friends for over ten years. In fact, she had met Kelly before she even knew Tim. Kelly had lived in her dorm at the University of North Carolina, and they had met in the cafeteria. Much to Angela's amazement—she had never dreamed she could have anything in common with an accounting major—they had become fast friends. Three years later, when the tiny business of computer games that Angela and Tim had started had grown so big that they needed someone to handle the accounts full-time, Angela had pulled Kelly into the business. Her levelheadedness had proved to be the perfect complement to Angela's and Tim's dreamer tendencies. Over the years, as their business had grown, so had Kelly's job; she presided over the entire business end of H & A Enterprises: orders, shipping, and accounting. Angela and Tim both agreed that whatever their creativity had produced, the business would never have boomed as it had without Kelly.

"Kelly..." Angela began thoughtfully, "why did you say you didn't think we needed Bryce's help?"

Kelly shrugged. "It seemed pretty clear to me that you didn't like him. That you didn't want him to be messing in our business records."

"You're right, I didn't." Angela got up and began to pace the room.

Her instinctive reaction had been to get rid of Bryce. But now she was beginning to wonder if she had acted in a hasty and childish manner. Her parents had been worried enough about her situation to send him—and whatever else one might say about the elder Hewitts, they knew the business world. They were not likely to panic or act impulsively; they were logical and coolly analytical to a fault. They also knew exactly how good Bryce Richards was at his business. If, in their opinion, he could help H & A Enterprises out of this trouble, then he probably could.

"Maybe I was wrong to kick him out so quickly," Angela admitted with a sigh. "Maybe I should have given him a chance to see if he could find anything."

"Your opinion is good enough for me," Tim responded, smiling at her reassuringly. "You know him better than Kelly and I do. I'm going to leave the decision up to you."

"I agree." Kelly chimed in.

"Thanks." Angela smiled at her friends. It warmed her heart that they had such confidence in her. People had told her that it would be impossible to be partners with a friend, but time had proven those doomsayers false. She had worked with Tim and Kelly for almost eight years, and both the business and their friendship had flourished.

Still, today was one time when she would have wished that they were not so quick to rely on her judgment. She was open-minded enough to admit that her dislike of Bryce was not rational, but emotional, and she worried now that she had made a mistake that might hurt their business.

Tim and Kelly returned to their offices, and Angela settled down behind her desk to work. But after several minutes of staring at her blank blue computer screen, she realized that working was impossible at the moment. Her mind was like a hamster on its wheel, circling endlessly.

With a sigh, she planted her elbows on the desk and sank her head onto her hands; she stared down at her desk, thinking. She disliked Bryce Richards, and she did not want him here at the office, poking his nose into everything. But, on the other hand, she would never forgive herself if he could have found the key to their financial troubles, and she had not let him just because of an old childhood antagonism.

Finally she picked up the phone and dialed her mother's number in Charlotte. A few minutes later, she was in her car heading toward the Radisson Hotel.

Two

Bryce leaned back in his chair and massaged his temples wearily. He had checked into his hotel and started work on his presentation for CompCon tomorrow, just as he had planned, but he found it difficult to concentrate on the numbers strung out across the sheets in front of him. His meeting with Angela had left him irritable and dissatisfied.

He made a noise of disgust and got to his feet. *That woman!* He got up and began to pace the room. Angela Hewitt was as great a pest as she had been as an adolescent. He could remember with great clarity the silly tricks she had played on him when he came to visit her mother. A slightly chubby girl with wild, curly red hair and a mouthful of braces, she had seemed to delight in making Bryce feel foolish and out of place. And, of course, he thought, remembering his own gawky, uncertain self, he had been the perfect foil for her tricks. He had already felt ill at ease just being in the Hewitts' house. It was gracious and obviously expensive, but without a breath of ostentation, a jewel of old-money taste. Being inside their house had been a glimpse into an entirely different sort of life for him, a life that he had wanted with every fiber of his being. At the same time, he had been terrified that he might break something in his awkwardness or that he might make some gauche mistake that would reveal his ignorance.

Angela seemed to have understood that with the instinct that children have, and she had played on it. Bryce had never been sure when he might find a whoopee cushion on his seat or a plastic bug in his drink. She was prone to tell him stories about her family, which he was never sure were true or not. He had believed the first one, that Angela's aunt was a famous pianist, and had mentioned something about her to Marina, who had looked at him blankly, then told him that she didn't have a sister. He had felt a fool and after that he was sure never to repeat anything Angela told him unless someone else had confirmed her story.

A reluctant smile twitched at Bryce's lips as he remembered her wilder concoctions. No one could ever accuse Angela of lacking imagination. Looking back on it now, he could see that her tricks were merely adolescent buffoonery. Someone with more confidence than he had at the time would have shrugged them off. But he had been a boy from the wrong side of the tracks, with nothing going for him but his brain, and he had wanted desperately to fit in.

Of course, he was nothing like that boy now. He was powerful and confident, used to moving in circles of great wealth. Coming down here, he had told himself that Angela had changed, too, that she would no longer get under his skin. After all, he simply would not allow it.

It had taken him less than five minutes to realize how wrong he had been. Angela Hewitt was as infuriating as ever. Oh, she had changed, all right—changed in a way that made his heart speed up and his loins begin to throb in a most annoying manner. The pudgy girl with a mouth of metal was gone; in her place was a curvaceous woman whose curling mass of red hair made a man want to sink his hands into it. Bryce had found that his eyes returned again and again to Angela's soft, high breasts—all too visible in that ridiculous costume she had been wearing—and his palms had itched with a desire to follow the curve of her buttocks. Even now he couldn't keep his mind off her full, soft mouth; his mind had drifted off his presentation figures several times to contemplate exactly how those lips would feel beneath his.

But that intense, vibrant desirability did not ease Bryce's irritation with her; if anything, it made it even worse. He hated the fact that he had responded physically to a woman who grated so on his nerves. Bryce had never been one who let his hungers intrude on his professional life. It was his policy never to date anyone with whom he worked—employee, boss, or client—and it was a policy from which he had never strayed. Oh, he would notice when a woman in his office or in one of his client's was exceptionally pretty or sexy. He was, after all, a man, and he was stirred by the sight of long, well-shaped legs or a deliciously curved figure. But it was never more than a passing thought. He noticed it, then dismissed it from his mind. Nor was he ever interested in a woman whom he disliked or who irritated him, at least not for longer than it took for her to get on his nerves.

But today, standing there with Angela Hewitt, irritated as he was by her obstructive, naive attitude, he couldn't keep his eyes off her, couldn't help thinking how delightful it would feel to have those legs twined around his back. It was disturbing to have been so attracted yet so annoyed by her. Bryce Richards did not like anything illogical, and his wayward thoughts about Angela certainly did not make sense.

It was just as well, he told himself, that she had not wanted his expertise. It would have been difficult working with the woman, given his conflicting emotions. He would be better off not being in her office—yet it was thoroughly exasperating to have her deny his offer of aid.

There was a knock on the door, and Bryce turned, relieved, thinking that it was room service. He had called them and ordered dinner a few minutes earlier. No doubt much of his turmoil and lack of ability to concentrate was due to the fact that he was hungry. Once he had eaten, he would feel like his old self again.

He opened the door, smiling in anticipation, only to find that the person outside his door was Angela Hewitt. His face fell in disappointment.

"Oh. It's you."

"Why, thank you," Angela returned sarcastically. "Nice to see you, too."

Bryce grimaced and stepped aside, motioning for her to enter. "I was expecting room service. Besides," he went on as she walked into the room, "our last meeting did not leave me with a great deal of eagerness to see you again.''

"For Heaven's sake..." Angela gave an airy wave of her hand and went to the window to look out at the view. "Can't anyone disagree with you without your holding a grudge?''

Bryce found himself watching the action of her hips beneath her tight jeans as she walked, and that irritated him as much as her words. He closed the door with a snap. "I'm not holding a grudge, I simply hoped I wouldn't have to see you again.''

Angela turned. "You're so stuffy. You were stuffy even when you were nineteen.''

"Yes, and you were a pest. I'm sorry to say that you haven't changed much, either.''

Angela lifted her chin in a defiant gesture. She hated apologizing—and to have to do it to this man, of all people! Gritting her teeth, she said, "I came to tell you that—that I was wrong. This afternoon when you were at our office, I was...''

"Rude?'' Bryce suggested.

Angela flashed him a disgusted look and said, "Abrupt. I should not have dismissed your help so peremptorily.''

"Your partners ganged up on you to accept?''

"No. In fact, Tim told me to do whatever I think is best. He and Kelly trust me, you see. However, when I thought about it, I realized that I wasn't acting in the company's best interest. I was simply reacting to—'' she made a vague gesture toward him "—the past. And my parents. I hate to accept help from them. It confirms their opinion of me.''

Bryce looked puzzled. "And what is their opinion of you?''

Angela gave him a look that indicated that she doubted his mental powers. "That I'm a flake. Ditzy and incompetent. All they see in any business is numbers, and they know how I am with those. So they figure that I'm bound to fail."

"I don't get that impression from them. I think they're rather proud of you and your success, actually."

Angela stared. "Are you sure you're talking about *my* parents? Everett and Marina Hewitt?"

A faint smile touched Bryce's lips. "Yes, I believe those are the ones."

"I think you're mistaken."

"No. I imagine I know them a lot better than you. They may not understand you or what you do—"

Angela let out a dry chuckle. "That's the understatement of all time."

"—but they love you and are very proud of you. That's why they're concerned about this problem with the IRS."

"Yes. My little problem." Angela made a disgusted face and turned away to gaze out the window again.

When it appeared that she was going to say nothing else, Bryce prompted, "How did you find me?"

"I called Mother. She told me you always stayed here when you were in Raleigh, and she said you planned to spend the night because you had a presentation to CompCon in the morning. They're a good company, by the way, but you have to handle Jason Willard with kid gloves."

He gave her a stiff little bow of his head. "Thank you for the advice."

"You're welcome," Angela replied, ignoring the note of sarcasm in his voice. She crossed her arms and looked at him.

Standing outside Bryce's door, her stomach had been jittery with nerves. But now, seeing the mulish expression on his face, Angela felt, perversely, more relaxed. Bryce obviously did not like her being here. That fact made it easier for her to admit that she needed his help.

"Anyway," she said, sitting down and crossing her legs, "I'm sorry. I thought about what you'd said, and Tim and Kelly and I talked it over. I decided I had been wrong to turn down your offer." She gazed up at him a little defiantly, more as if she were being scolded than admitting that she had made a mistake. Bryce found it strangely appealing.

"I came to ask you if your offer still held," she said. "Are you willing to find our problem?"

Angela could see from his face that he would have liked to turn her down, but she was counting on his promise to her mother to keep him from doing what he wanted.

Finally, grudgingly, he said, "Yes. I suppose I am— though, God knows, I'll probably regret it. I can imagine what your records are like. You probably keep all your invoices in a shoe box."

Angela grinned impishly. "I'd love to tell you that they were, just to see the smoke come out of your ears, but I can't malign Kelly. She keeps excellent records. She's not at all like me."

"Obviously."

Angela made a face at him. She watched him, more relaxed now that she had choked out her apology. She wondered why she had not remembered how handsome he was. Even if he had filled out, surely the bare bones of his good looks had been there: the firm, well-cut lips, the strong bones of his face, the dark-lashed gray eyes.

Bryce walked over to the table and sat down across from her. Angela could see the wary look on his face, and she wondered what he thought she was going to do. She decided not to help him out. She gazed back at him with wide eyes, swinging her foot and waiting for him to make the first move.

"All right," he said, taking out a yellow pad and pencil and settling down to take notes. "Let's get some basics. I need to know about your business."

"Mother didn't tell you?"

"She said only that you made computer games."

"That's right. Fantasy sort of games, mostly, some flight and road simulation sort of things. We're beginning to move into the CD-Rom area. Our mainstay and what we started out with are the Concordia games and others like them."

"Concordia games?" Bryce raised his eyebrows.

"You've never heard of them?"

"I don't play computer games. I use my computer for work."

"Of course. How silly of me." Angela's smile flashed, creating a dimple in her cheek.

There was something definitely sexy, Angela thought, about Bryce's serious, intense gaze. The silvery gray eyes seemed to go right through her. She wondered if he brought the same single-minded intensity to his lovemaking as he did to his work. The thought sent a shiver through her.

She glanced away from him quickly. She couldn't believe that she was thinking about Bryce this way.

Bryce Richards, of all people! It was crazy; they could hardly manage to string together three or four civil sentences to each other. The thought of ever going to bed with him was sheer insanity. He was not her type, and she felt sure that Bryce would run as fast as he could the other way if he thought that she was interested in him. He had made it very clear what he thought of her.

"The Concordia games are quest games," she said quickly to get her mind off her strange thoughts. "They are set in a fictional kingdom, Concordia, in some past time, vaguely medieval. There's a king and queen and their beautiful daughter, Princess Alicia. Their enemy is an evil sorceress, Maladora."

"Ah!" Bryce's brows flew up in a look of enlightenment. "That's who you were dressed as this afternoon."

"Yeah."

"Why?"

"Oh. For Tim's party...it's a week from Friday. A big charity costume party he throws every year for this children's charity he's involved with."

"Oh." His face cleared. "Okay. So what does this Maladora do?"

"Anyway, Maladora is very powerful, and though, of course, she's defeated in each game, she always finds some way of coming back. In a weird way, people are probably more attached to her than to the princess or even Sir Leopold. He's the knight from another country who came to Concordia and released the royal family from the enchantment that Maladora had put them under. That was our first game, *Concordia.* Our second was *Concordia: Maladora Returns* and the third was *Concordia: Alicia's Escape,* and so on. Right now I'm working on the seventh. I'm going to introduce a new villain and have Maladora on the same side as the royal family for once. The games are humorous, particularly the contemporary series. We always put in little tongue-in-cheek things. They're not the violent ones where you kick and stab and shoot your way to the end—you win by figuring out clues and collecting things along the way, then using them at the right time."

"I see."

From the expression on his face, Angela doubted that he did, but she let it pass. Bryce, she suspected, simply didn't understand games; they were beyond his scope. That was the way her parents were. Numbers made sense; fantasies and entertainment did not.

"And these games are successful?"

"Very." Angela bit back a smile at the faint tone of amazement in his voice. "People love them. They're interesting and complex—you can work on them for days. One gets fun and a sense of accomplishment out of them. That big open room downstairs in our office, the one that has all the little cubicles with people with headsets?"

He nodded, remembering glancing into the room.

"Those are our telephone support lines. People who buy the games call to get help in using them. The support staff help customers if they're having trouble setting up, and if they're stuck, they'll give them hints and ideas. The support lines are busy all day long. We're grossing millions."

Bryce looked faintly shocked. Angela supposed that from her mother's explanation, he had expected Angela to have some little shoestring operation.

"How is the company set up?" he asked, scribbling on the pad.

"It's a corporation. Tim and I started out as partners, but when it got bigger, we incorporated. Tim and I own nearly all the shares."

"Kelly's not a partner?"

"No. She's bought some shares, and all our employees have gotten some shares as bonuses, but basically Tim and I own it. We began it. Later, we hired Kelly to do our accounting. Her job has grown as we have. Basically, now she oversees all operations except creating the games."

"You and Tim do that?"

"Yes. I think up the stories and write out the plot line. Tim creates the software for them. We each have a few assistants now, but we still pretty much do all the Concordia games ourselves." She shrugged. "It's a lot more fun than overseeing the other stuff. I leave the simulation games alone. That's Jeremy Coger's field."

She went on to explain how the games were packaged, marketed and distributed, and all the while Bryce scribbled across his pad. Angela looked at his hand as it moved across the page. His skin was tanned, the back of his hand and his fingers lightly dotted with curling dark hairs. His fingers were long and strong, the nails short-clipped. It was a very masculine, no-nonsense sort of hand, but not stubby or rough. It wasn't hard to imagine it moving with gentleness across a woman's body.

Suddenly Angela's thoughts flew to the bed beside them. She had hardly noticed it when she came in, but now it seemed to fill the room. She kept her eyes firmly away from it, sure that Bryce would somehow guess her thoughts if she so much as glanced at it. But, of course, since she was determined not to look at it, looking at it became an almost impossible urge to resist. She jumped restlessly to her feet and began to pace.

There was a long moment of silence, and Angela pivoted to look at Bryce. He was watching her, his brow drawn into a frown. She frowned back.

"Well? Are we through?"

He started and looked disconcerted. "What? Oh. No, I . . . let's see." He turned back to his yellow pad. "What about the IRS? When did that start?"

"About three months ago. They called us in for a routine audit. We showed them our records, and I assumed that was the last of it. Then all of a sudden, they started asking more questions, nosing around. I don't know what they saw that set them off. This one guy, McGuire, kept saying that we didn't make enough profit—like it was some kind of crime or something. We didn't make as much profit as the last few years. But we just had a lot more expenses. Things like that happen. Don't they?"

"Sure. And the IRS could be off track. Unfortunately they usually manage to run something down."

Angela sighed. "I'm beginning to feel paranoid."

"The IRS can do that to you."

"I tell myself that if we haven't done anything wrong, we don't have anything to worry about. But they're making me jittery. I keep thinking that somewhere we must have made a mistake and I just can't see it. That's why I told Mother the other day. I shouldn't have . . . I knew it would worry her."

"I'm sure she was glad you told her. She wants to help you."

"I know. And she always expects that she'll have to. That's what makes it so galling." Angela grimaced. "I hate to screw up in front of her."

Bryce looked amazed. "But Marina's very patient and understanding about mistakes. That's why she's such a wonderful teacher."

"Yeah, well, it's probably different when you're a student rather than her daughter. When I didn't understand things in math, she acted like I was being purposely obstructive. She couldn't believe that I didn't get it. Finally she came to realize that I really didn't understand these things that seemed so obvious to her. Then she'd get this—I don't know, *distressed* sort of look in her eyes. And I'd know that I disappointed her. I think she was afraid that I was mentally impaired."

"Don't be ridiculous," Bryce said gruffly.

Angela glared at him. *How could she have forgotten that she was talking to the man who thought Marina Hewitt could do no wrong?* "I wouldn't have expected you to understand."

"Your prejudice is appalling." He got up and strode across the room to where she stood.

"I'm not prejudiced!" Angela retorted, stung.

"I'm sure you're not about all the politically correct things, but you most definitely are about people who are logical or mathematical. You presume that if a person understands numbers, they don't understand anything else, that they're emotionless robots. Being logical doesn't mean that you can't understand feelings."

"You, I'm sure, are in touch with your feelings." It galled her for him to lecture her, as if she were still a child.

"What is that supposed to mean?"

"It means you're too stiff and uptight to even know that you have feelings. Look at you . . . here it is . . . six o'clock, in your hotel room, and you're still wearing a tie—knotted at the top! I'm surprised you even took off your suit jacket. You were the same when you were nineteen, too. Stiff, dry, logical. You looked at my friends and me playing in the pool like we were creatures from another planet. And when I played a joke on you, you never even got mad. Any normal person would have blown up, but you just got stiffer and quieter. No doubt it wasn't logical to get mad."

Bryce stared at her in disbelief. "What should I have done? Tell my hostess's child what a spoiled brat she was? Of course I held my tongue. To have said anything would have been hurtful to Marina. No doubt you think it's ridiculous to be courteous."

"Of course not!" Red flamed in Angela's cheeks. She felt foolish and embarrassed and oddly hurt by his opinion of her. "But you can be courteous and still be capable of human emotions. You don't have to be a statue like you."

Bryce knew that was how she saw him, as a bloodless, passionless person, more a wax figure than a man. The idea infuriated him, all the more so because right now his blood was thrumming through his veins and even as they fought he could not stop thinking how desirable she looked. Angela was thoroughly annoying, but some elemental instinct in him wanted her, and that fact was as irritating as she was.

Suddenly, surprising himself as much as her, Bryce reached out and grabbed her shoulders. Angela froze in astonishment, staring at him with wide, disbelieving eyes as he pulled her to him and took her mouth in a long, searing kiss.

His lips were hot and demanding; his tongue slid along the seal of her lips, seeking entrance. Angela shivered, her knees amazingly weak, and opened her mouth to his seeking tongue. It was not a sweet kiss; it burned with anger and resentment . . . and passion. There was nothing emotionless or saintly about him now. His body curved around hers, his arms pressing her into his hard chest and thighs, and the heat was enveloping, enervating. His mouth possessed hers as if by right, his tongue exploring, challenging.

Angela sagged against him, and her fingers dug into his shirt in the back as she clung to him. His kiss made her tremble, made her forget who he was and what he was to her. She tasted the driving hunger that aroused her own, and she wanted more. Her tongue wound around his, stroking and seeking. She felt his breath shuddering out, hot upon her cheek, and his kiss gentled, no longer demanding, but coaxing and enticing her. His hand stroked up and down her back, pressing her into him. Angela wrapped her arms around his neck and gave herself up to his kiss.

Three

Bryce's lips moved over Angela's, deliciously firm and warm. His hand slid down her body and onto her hip, then slowly back up. His thumb brushed against the side of her breast, sending a quiver of desire through her abdomen.

He lifted his mouth, but only to change the slant of his kiss. His kiss deepened; his tongue invaded her mouth. Angela answered eagerly, tasting the dark, silky pleasures of his mouth. She felt weak and strangely helpless, not like herself at all, but somehow the feeling was pleasurable as well as scary, as if she were about to step onto a wild ride at an amusement park or enter a new adventure. She wrapped her arms around Bryce's neck, clinging to him.

For a long moment they were lost in intense pleasure, their mouths locked together, their bodies straining against each other. Then there was a knock on the door, breaking into the enchantment, and a bored voice drawled, "Room Service."

Angela jumped, startled, and her lip came into painful contact with Bryce's teeth. She stepped back, one hand pressed to her smarting lip, and stared at Bryce dazedly. *This couldn't be happening. Bryce Richards had just kissed her—and she had enjoyed it.*

"Room service," the disembodied voice repeated outside the door, and Bryce jerked into movement.

"Yes. Coming." He started toward the door.

Angela cast a wild look around the room, then sank into a chair, pushing her hands back into her thick, curling hair. She tried to pull her thoughts back into some semblance of order while Bryce dealt with the hotel employee.

She had done some impulsive things in her life, but it occurred to her that this was probably the worst. *Bryce Richards disliked her; he hadn't kissed her because he was attracted to her. He had done it because she had made him mad. He had done it to establish that he was in control, to prove her wrong. She had insulted him, more or less accused him of being without passion, and he, of course, had to show her that he was not.*

And she, like an idiot, had responded to his kiss! Angela couldn't imagine what was wrong with her that she had acted that way. He was handsome, of course— *in a cold way,* she reminded herself—but he was all the things she disliked in a man: a staid workaholic with no sense of humor, a man who did things only because they made sense. She could not imagine Bryce Richards skipping a day of work to go out and have a picnic. He was the sort of man who would bring a woman flowers because that was the accepted thing to do, but he would never think of surprising her with some odd little present that had irresistibly reminded him of her. He would make plans for an evening and follow them to the letter. In short, he was the sort of man with whom she would be bored in an hour or two—no matter how much she might feel an utterly inexplicable physical attraction to him.

It also occurred to Angela that right now Bryce was probably regretting what he had just done just as much as she was. She looked up.

Bryce was shutting the door behind the waiter. He turned and gazed across the room at her, every line of his body screaming that he was uncomfortable. He cleared his throat. "Well . . ."

Angela popped to her feet. "I better be going now."

"What? Oh, yes, I suppose so. Look, Angela, I'm sorry—"

She shook her head, putting on what she hoped was a cheery, nonchalant face. "Nonsense. Happens to me all the time. Men stop me on the street to kiss me. It's my irresistible charm."

She nodded and left the room, closing the door behind her.

Bryce stood still for a moment after she left, gazing blankly at the door. Finally he turned to the room service cart and absently lifted the covers. His earlier hunger had vanished, and he studied the food with uninterest.

Room service had come just in time, he thought. *Who knows what might have happened if they had not been interrupted?*

Stifling a sigh, he sat down and began to eat.

* * *

Angela drove home in a fury. She parked her car in the single garage assigned to her condominium and stomped up the stairs to her condo, still seething over her encounter with Bryce Richards.

The condominium complex where she lived was small and secluded, surrounded by large, spreading oaks. It was an elegant place without being pretentious, and its occupants were by and large young professionals without children. Angela's condo, toward the rear of the complex, was a small, utilitarian, down-to-earth place with little decoration. She didn't spend much time here. Her real home was the lake house, and it was there that she had put in most of her effort of furnishing and decorating. This condo was simply a place to sleep during the week, and its primary advantages were that it was quiet and close to work.

The furniture was simple and comfortable; some of it she had had from the tiny first apartment she had shared with Kelly when their business was beginning. It looked old and well lived-in, and the stacks of books all around—in bookcases, on tables and in piles on the floor—added to the casual, cozy ambience. At odds with the furniture, however, were the array of electronic machines and gadgets around the place.

Angela had always been intrigued by gadgets and time-saving or energy-saving devices, and when the company had started making good money, she had allowed herself to indulge in the clever machines that caught her fancy. Though she was not fond of cooking, her kitchen was a treasure trove of bread machines, cappuccino makers, electric steamers, ice-cream machines and various sorts of food processors. The second bedroom, which served as her office at home, was stocked with a fax machine, copier, two computers and an assortment of hand-held computerized games, translators, calculators and electronic novelties. Her favorite was the home theater setup at one end of her living room, where a large-screen TV and a multitude of speakers, VCRs, laser disc players, tuners, tape players, etc., provided sensational sound and view for any movie.

Tonight, however, she had no interest in popping any cassette into the VCR. Nor did cooking a dinner appeal to her. She was too restless, too agitated; her mind kept jumping from her tax troubles to Bryce Richards to her bizarre behavior in his hotel room. She rattled purposelessly around the condo for a few minutes and finally wound up on the small balcony in back.

The balcony was shielded from the sun and neighbors by large, sheltering oaks, but it had a clear view of the balcony next door. There a slim, curly-haired, middle-aged man fussed over a group of hanging plants, watering them and carefully breaking off dead leaves.

"Hi, Jim." Angela leaned against the railing and smiled at the man, who turned and beamed at her. Jim had more or less adopted Angela when she first moved into her condo six years earlier, telling her she was the daughter he had never had, and they had weathered many an emotional storm with each other over the intervening years.

"Sweetheart!" He came over, the empty watering pot dangling from his hand. "My, aren't you home early? What happened?"

Angela grimaced reflexively. "Trouble, probably."

"Really?" His brows arched in amused curiosity. "Do tell. Is it interesting or some boring business thing?"

"It's people, not business. Or maybe a combination of both."

"Well, why don't you come over and tell Daddy all about it? I have hot water on the stove and I'll fix you a nice cup of herbal tea if you want."

"Sure. That sounds great." Angela turned and walked back through her condominium.

Jim opened the door for her just as she reached it and led her inside, chattering all the way as he walked back into the kitchen to fetch her tea.

His condo was a mirror image of hers structurally, but there would never be any mistaking the two. Jim's place was done in the same campy, flamboyant style in which he spoke and acted. Having been around him in moments when he was quite serious, direct, and even practical, Angela had never been quite sure whether this flamboyance was real or merely something he assumed as befitting the owner of a trendy art gallery.

"So what happened?" he asked as he bustled back out of the kitchen, carrying a small tray on which sat two cups.

Angela, who had kicked off her shoes and leaned back in an ultramodern turquoise canvas chair, reached up and took the steaming cup gratefully. "Mmm . . . smells delicious."

"Thank you. I had water heated because I was expecting Harbaugh, but, of course, he called about two minutes before you came and said he was going to be late again. Lawyers." He made a face and took a sip of his tea. "But never mind that. Tell me about you."

Angela sighed and began to relate the events of this afternoon, to Jim's appreciative noises and comments. When she finished, she shrugged. "So there you have it. I dislike this guy, always have. He represents everything I don't like about my family and that whole world they inhabit. And then all of a sudden, he kissed me! And I enjoyed it!"

"Sounds like not such a terrible problem to me," Jim joked.

Angela answered with a derisive snort. "I'm serious. It's a complication, a stupid, weird complication—as if I didn't have enough with this IRS thing hanging over my head."

"Well, you know, opposites attract and all that. I mean, look at Harbaugh and me—a lawyer, for pity's sake! You know how serious he is. Sometimes I swear the man has no sense of humor. But we've been together almost four years now."

"I know. With some people it probably works out. But you don't know Bryce Richards. He's not just serious or humorless, he's also methodical and critical and analytical. I doubt that the man knows how to have fun. Everything has to have a reason. Besides, we don't even like each other. He's precisely the type of man I don't want, and I'm sure he still has some kind of grudge against me, considering all the awful twelve-year-old kind of practical jokes I played on him. I mean, just because I've grown up and suddenly there's this physical thing between us, that doesn't mean that we're going to start liking each other. We're still the same people, like night and day. It would be a mess . . . especially with us working together now. It's going to be hard enough being in the same office with him as it is. If we were having an affair, too, it would be impossible.''

"Sorry," Jim said, retreating into the serious persona that he usually strove to keep hidden. "Just teasing—although it does sound like there's an awful lot of free-floating emotions in this relationship. Well, frankly, Angie, it seems to me like the only solution is to avoid him.''

"How can I do that? He'll be working right down the hall from me.''

"So? Go to work late and stay late. You already do that lots of times. Stay in your office while you're there and don't go wandering all over talking to everybody.''

"Exile myself from my own business?'' Angela frowned. "I don't want to do that.''

"Then get rid of him.''

"No. That wouldn't be fair to Tim and Kelly. We need his help even if I don't like him.'' Angela sighed. "I guess you're right. I'll try to avoid him as much as I possibly can. I'll hide out in my office till he's through.'' She smiled at him. "Thanks.''

"Ah, it was nothing.'' Jim made a dismissive gesture with his hand.

"Of course it was. Herbal tea and advice—what more could a person ask for?''

Jim rolled his eyes comically. "Lots.''

"Well, it's enough for tonight. I appreciate your listening to me. But let's talk about something more interesting now. How's your new show coming?''

"Oh, my dear!'' Jim clasped his hand to his chest dramatically and proceeded to launch into a long description of his latest trials and tribulations with the

temperamental but talented artist whose work he was
about to exhibit in his gallery.

Angela stuck to her decision to avoid Bryce at the
office. She came to work late the next day and walked
the long way around to her office door in order to
avoid passing Kelly's office, where Bryce was working. She kept her door resolutely closed all day, and
she got their receptionist to buy her a sandwich and
bring it up to her office on her lunch hour.

She felt foolish, as if she were a child playing hooky
and hiding from authority. Worse than that, she found
that she spent so much time listening for Bryce's voice
or footsteps in the hall and wondering whether he
would come knock on her office door that she got almost no work done.

Late the next afternoon, when most of the employees had left, she started down to the kitchen to get a
snack to sustain her, but when she opened her door,
she spotted Kelly and Bryce walking along the hallway toward her, deep in conversation. Quickly she
ducked back into her office and listened as they
walked past. She waited several more minutes, then
cautiously opened her door and peeked out. No one
was in the hall. She walked quickly and quietly down
the hallway to the stairs.

Downstairs, she peeked out the front door and saw
that the black Mercedes sedan Bryce had parked there
this morning was gone. With a sigh of relief, she went
into the kitchen and began to rummage around for
something to eat. In accordance with the casual way
they did everything here at H & A Enterprises, most
of the workers brought in food from time to time and,
unless it was boldly labeled, whatever was there was

generally considered fair game. Tim usually kept them generously supplied with soft drinks, and Dorothy Fairfax, the receptionist, made such good desserts that Tim and Angela reimbursed her so that she would bring them regularly.

Angela checked the plastic-wrapped pan on the counter first and sighed with disappointment to find that Dorothy's brownies had been demolished. She settled for a container of peach yogurt from the refrigerator and put a cup of water in the microwave to heat for tea. She sat at the table, absently spooning the yogurt into her mouth and gazing out at the quiet yard as the day drifted slowly into dusk. She wondered what Bryce had done that day.

There were familiar footsteps in the wooden hallway outside, and Angela turned, a smile already spreading across her face. "Hi, Kelly."

"Oh, hi!" Kelly looked a little surprised. "I didn't know you were here. I thought you left a long time ago. Your door was closed all afternoon."

"No. I was in my office working."

"Oh. The new game?" Kelly pulled a soft drink out of the refrigerator and plopped down at the table across from Angela.

"Yeah." Angela didn't think it was necessary to add that she had gotten almost nothing done on the project.

"Sorry. I told Bryce you were gone."

"He wanted to see me?" Angela looked at her sharply.

"He was going to say goodbye."

"Goodbye?" Angela's eyebrows vaulted upward. Something strangely like panic seized her chest. "He's left? I mean, gone back to Charlotte? Already?"

"Well, just for a few days. He told me what he wants to look at when he comes back, so I'm getting the records printed up for him. In the meantime, he's gone back to Charlotte to tie up some things there. He said he'd be back here Monday."

"Oh. Of course." Angela looked down into her empty yogurt container, busily scraping the remains of the creamy stuff off the sides and bottom of the cup, as she asked casually, "What did he do today?"

"Not much. Sort of familiarized himself with our system. Asked me a bunch of questions about how the business office is run and who has access to what. Internal security sort of things. Apparently he thinks we're pretty sloppy."

Angela snorted indelicately. "*He'd* probably accuse St. Peter of keeping sloppy accounts."

Kelly chuckled. "You're too hard on him. He seems like a nice guy. Very polite." She paused, then added, "Not to mention cute."

"Cute?" Angela wrinkled her nose. "Puppies are cute. Bryce Richards is not cute."

"All right. Handsome, then. What is it with you two?"

"What do you mean?"

"Well, you hired him, and he's a friend of your family's. But you keep making cracks about him. And he keeps asking questions about you—not all of which are what I would consider business-related—but when I suggested that he ask you some of those questions instead of me, he turned all stiff and wouldn't do it. So what's the deal?"

Angela shrugged. "There's no deal. We've known each other since I was twelve, and he is good friends with my mother and father, but the two of us never hit it off. We're complete opposites. He's totally anal and obsessive."

Kelly laughed. "He said you were—I believe it was unrealistic and impractical."

"That's typical." Angela got up and went to the microwave to take out her cup and plop the tea bag in it. "I guess he's not bad, really. He's just so into numbers and things. You know." She turned and grinned at her friend. "You might like him, actually. At least you could understand what he talks about. I never could. Maybe you could even get him to lighten up a little."

"I don't think he'd be interested in me," Kelly retorted. "I got the distinct impression that it's you he's got a thing for."

"Got a thing for?" Angela repeated disbelievingly. "Uh-uh. Believe me, I am not his type. He's so uptight and correct he probably wears pajamas to bed— with little paisley patterns all over them." She paused, then added, "Ironed pajamas. Starched."

Kelly chuckled and said, "Then why did he keep looking toward your office every time he went out into the hall today if he isn't interested in you?"

"He's probably trying to avoid me—like I was trying to avoid him."

Kelly studied her thoughtfully, then went on. "Okay. Tell me this . . . why is it necessary for you all to try so hard to do that? Hmm? I mean, I think it'd come naturally to two people who didn't like each other."

With that parting shot, Kelly left the kitchen, throwing a last teasing glance over her shoulder as she walked out the door. Angela grimaced as she picked up her cup and followed her. Kelly had been teasing her, she told herself. There was no basis for what she had said. She and Bryce had succumbed to some strange quirk of passion last night. It didn't mean that he had any real interest in her. And, certainly, she was not interested in him!

Four

With Bryce gone, Angela's work progressed more quickly. It surprised her a little since for the two or three weeks before this her brain seemed to have been stuck. Every time she had tried to concentrate on the plot for the new game, her mind had willfully gone back to worrying over their tax situation. Now, however, it didn't intrude. Reluctant as she was to admit it, she realized finally that she must have confidence that Bryce would find the problem and handle it, and she was able to relax and return to her work.

Friday afternoon, Angela again stayed at the office after the others had gone. She often worked after hours, as it was much easier without the noise and distractions of the day. Often Tim or Kelly or one of the others worked late as well. Theirs was a loose sort of business where workers more or less set their own hours.

Tonight Angela was by herself in the office. Kelly had a date, and Tim and his family had gone to the beach for the weekend. Angela's fingers flew over the computer keyboard as she expanded her ideas. Over the past hour, she had been growing gradually more aware that she was hungry, but she was too deeply involved in the creative process to stop and get something to eat.

Finally, however, a harsh metallic clang intruded on her consciousness, and she looked up from her computer screen. *What in the world had that been?* Her heart picked up its beat. She knew that there should be no one else in the office, especially up here on the second floor, which was primarily her, Tim's and Kelly's domain. She thought about burglars. There was never much cash in their office, but they did have lots of expensive electronic equipment—and not just equipment, either; Tim's office was full of all the games he loved and their paraphernalia.

Angela stood up and tiptoed to the door into the hallway to peer out cautiously. Light slanted out of Kelly's open door into the hallway. Angela's heart began to race. She knew that Kelly had left almost three hours earlier. There was no reason why anyone should be in her office—and Kelly's door was always locked, since many of their records were kept there. That meant whoever was there would have had to break in.

Angela glanced back at the telephone on her desk and wondered if she should call 911. But somehow she could not quite believe that someone had really broken in, and she thought of how stupid she would feel if she called 911 and they came charging in only to find that Kelly's date had been broken at the last minute and she had decided to come work off her irritation.

Angela stood for a moment indecisively then tiptoed back to her desk and picked up the large piece of mahogany obsidian that she used as a paperweight. Hefting it in one hand, she sneaked out the door and down the hall, careful not to make a sound. At Kelly's door, she peeked around the doorframe. She could see nothing except Kelly's desk, the desk lamp casting a golden circle of light over it. Angela leaned farther in, her head craning around to see behind Kelly's desk.

On the other side of Kelly's office, hidden by the open door, a file drawer banged against its metal frame as it rolled in. Angela jumped, an involuntary gasp escaping her, and the heavy rock slipped from her hand. It hit the floor with a loud thud.

"What the hell!"

Angela froze. There were footsteps and an instant later, a man's hand swung the door all the way open. Bryce Richards stepped into the doorway.

"Oh. It's you," they chorused.

Angela let out her breath and pressed her hand against her chest, where her heart was pounding crazily.

"What the hell did you do?" Bryce asked, and his gaze fell to the rock on the floor between them. "Did you drop that?"

Angela nodded.

He looked at her as if she might be deranged. "What were you doing carrying a rock around?"

Angela stiffened. "I thought you might be a burglar. So I picked up my paperweight before I came to investigate. What do you think I should have done, come without anything to protect myself?"

"If you thought I was a burglar, the smart thing would have been to stay in your office and call the police."

"Well, then we'd have looked pretty silly, wouldn't we?" she retorted.

He shrugged. "Better silly than shot by a startled thief."

He bent and picked up the chunk of dark rock flecked with red and handed it back to her with a mockly formal bow. Angela grimaced and cradled the rock in the crook of her arm.

"What are *you* doing here?" she asked ungraciously. "I thought you were in Charlotte the rest of the week."

"I was. But I finished early this afternoon, so I thought I'd drive down and get started. This weekend'll be a good time to work. Nobody around. It'll take less time away from my business. And Kelly had given me her spare set of keys."

It irritated Angela that Bryce seemed to view her business's problem as something to do in his spare time, not his real "business."

"I take it you don't believe in taking time off?" she asked tartly.

Bryce cocked an eyebrow and asked pointedly, "And what are you doing here?"

Angela flushed, but said, "It's easier to work now when it's quiet."

"I rest my case."

"I'm *not* a workaholic," Angela went on defensively. "I simply set different hours from some people. I come to work late."

Bryce grinned unexpectedly and said, "It's okay for you to work late. I'm not accusing you of anything."

Angela glared back at him, annoyed. She was the one who had been acting unreasonably, sniping at him for working after hours as if it were some kind of crime, yet she couldn't help feeling that for some reason she needed to defend herself. Bryce Richards had that effect on her. She always felt guilty and in the wrong around him. Grimacing, she turned on her heel and started back toward her office.

"Wait."

Angela turned. Bryce was standing in the doorway of the office, frowning after her. "What?"

"Would you tell me something?"

She shrugged. "I suppose."

"What is it exactly that you have against me? You asked me to work on this for you, if you'll remember. I didn't force you."

"Of course not." Angela squirmed mentally. "I didn't mean to be…well, I'm just a little irritable this evening. I've probably been working too long today."

"It isn't just today. It's been the same since I met you when you were twelve years old. You took an instant dislike to me, and you've never changed your opinion."

Angela was at a loss for words. She simply stared at him, guilt washing over her. Bryce was right. She had been terrible to him when she was younger. Even if he had been stiff and rather priggish, he hadn't deserved all her childish pranks. And her own unhappiness wasn't a sufficient excuse for the way she had acted.

"I—I'm sorry," she said finally, her gaze dropping.

"You needn't apologize. I simply wondered."

"Yes, I do need to apologize." Angela raised her eyes to him. "I was a perfect rat to you back when I was a kid. I'm sure you must have hated me."

A smile quirked up the corner of his mouth. "I was not overly fond of you, no." He leaned his shoulder against the doorjamb and crossed his arms. "But I suppose most adolescents are pests."

"Not like I was. You probably won't believe this, but nowadays I'm generally considered a nice person. Back then I was—I don't know—unhappy, bitter. And I took it out on you. I shouldn't have." She smiled faintly. "That's probably why I've been less than pleasant to you this time, too. The minute I saw you, all those old, bad feelings rose in me. As well as guilt for the way I'd treated you. I'm sorry, both for then and now."

"Apology accepted."

"Well..." Angela took a deep breath. "I feel better now. Got the monkey off my back. I tell you what. I'm starving. Why don't I take you out for some food—an olive branch, so to speak."

Surprise flitted across his face, but he said only, "Sure. That sounds good."

"Great." Angela grinned impishly. "Just let me take my rock back to my office and get my keys, and we'll go."

She returned a few moments later to find Bryce waiting, the suit jacket, which he had taken off earlier was once again in place, along with his tie.

Angela smothered a grin. Bryce obviously was not in tune with the casual life-style of their office. "We aren't going anywhere fancy," she said, reaching over and tugging the lapel of his jacket.

He shrugged. "I've worn a suit so many years I guess I feel uncomfortable without it."

Angela bit back the instinctive biting remark that rose to her lips, reminding herself that she had decided to make peace with Bryce. She was no longer the lonely, bitter girl she had once been. She was mature and could make a new judgment about the man, forget the old prejudices and dislikes.

Bryce followed Angela down the stairs and out into the parking lot. He cast a doubtful glance at her sporty red Miata, but he climbed into it gamely. He even kept his lips firmly closed as she zipped in and out of traffic, driving with her usual speed, verve and skill. Still, he looked relieved when they reached the restaurant and stopped.

The restaurant was in an old house in the University area, and except for the bold peach color of its walls and the green accents of its trim, Bryce would have taken it for a home. There was no sign proclaiming its name in front.

As soon as they walked in the front door, a tall, thin man with a balding head greeted Angela gleefully. "Angela Hewitt! Carrie and I were just talking about you today. Said you hadn't been in for a month. We thought maybe you'd crossed us off your list."

"Don't be a dope," Angela responded, giving the thin man a hug. "It's only been a couple of weeks, anyway."

She turned toward Bryce, saying, "Max, here's somebody I want you to meet—Bryce Richards. He's here from Charlotte. A friend of my parents. Bryce, this is Maxwell Janco, the owner of this fine establishment."

"Co-owner," the man corrected. "Eileen'd rip your heart out if she heard you slighted her." He reached out and shook Bryce's hand firmly. "Nice to meet you."

"It's a pleasure to meet you, Mr. Janco."

"Hey, call me Max. Everybody does."

Max beamed at Bryce. He reminded Bryce of a crane, with his tall, thin frame, and the jeans and old white T-shirt that he wore only accentuated his thinness. His bony, pale feet were laced into sandals that looked as if they'd come straight out of the Bible. Perhaps in compensation for his incipient baldness, he wore his dark hair long in back, catching it up in a ponytail in the back of his head. He had twinkling dark eyes, and the lower half of his face was dominated by a long, luxuriant, old-fashioned handlebar mustache, waxed into an amazing upward curl. He was, Bryce thought, one of the oddest-looking creatures he had ever met, certainly nothing like how he envisioned the owner or host of a restaurant.

"You want a table on the patio?" Max asked Angela, picking up a couple of menus and beginning to amble toward a door in the back wall.

"You know me," Angela replied. "I love the patio."

"You'll have it all to yourself tonight," Max said, agreeably.

Personally Bryce had little enthusiasm for eating outdoors; he saw no reason to have to wave away bugs and listen to traffic on the street while eating his food. However, he held his tongue. He wasn't about to spoil the fragile peace between him and Angela tonight.

And when Max led them onto the small wooden deck, tucked away from the street behind the house and further protected from noise by a high wall on one side, Bryce had to admit that it was a cozy and charming place to eat. There was greenery all around the small, intimate tables. Flowering plants hung from the overhead latticework, and ivy cascaded down the protective wall. On the two open sides, small shrubs edged the patio, and low lights scattered through the side yard gave one a view of a dainty garden, complete with goldfish pool. Discreet lighting placed here and there around the poles and latticework ceiling lent the patio a soft, romantic air.

"Very attractive," Bryce said politely as Max left them.

"I think so. It's my favorite restaurant. And the food is simply wonderful."

Bryce opened his menu and began to skim down the selections. He had been growing hungrier by the second as they drove over here. His eyes ran the list of salads, pastas and vegetable casseroles. He stopped and looked more carefully at each section. There were no steaks, no roast beefs, not even a hamburger, unless one counted the Soyburger Eileen. He looked back up at Angela warily.

"Is everything here vegetarian?"

Angela nodded. "Yes. They have dishes with eggs and cheeses in them, though."

"But no meat."

"No. But it's great . . . it really is. The Greek salad is scrumptious."

"Actually, I had something a little more substantial in mind."

"Well, they have heartier meals, too. This vegetable and brown rice casserole is really filling. Or the veggie fajitas." She paused and asked tentatively, "I'm sorry, I didn't think. Are you very opposed to meatless dishes?''

"No. I can live." A wry smile quirked the corner of his mouth. "I should have known you were into health food."

"Well, actually, I'm not a vegetarian. I even eat hamburgers, which drives Eileen crazy."

At that moment the door onto the patio opened, and a large woman rushed out, followed more sedately by a waitress carrying a water pitcher and order tablet. The woman was tall; Bryce judged her to be close to six feet, and she was built like a Valkyrie. She wore a loose patterned dress that fell to her ankles and shoes similar to her husband's. Her hair was black and shot through with a single dramatic streak of white, and she wore it fastened into a long, thick braid hanging almost down to her waist. A necklace of tiny bells jangled on her ample bosom.

"Angela!"

"Eileen." Angela jumped to her feet and went forward to greet the other woman. Eileen hugged Angela enthusiastically.

"I haven't seen you in ages."

"Two weeks," Angela protested faintly.

The other woman waved her words away. "You came to eat here. But you haven't been to the house in at least two months. Judy and Bean miss you."

She went on prattling about Judy and Bean and how much they had been pining away for Angela and how often they asked for her. Bryce took the pair to be her children, until Angela laughed and said, "You expect me to believe that? The last time I came over to visit, Judy took off like a streak at the sight of me and hung from inside the chimney swinging her tail."

"Well, that's because it had been so long since you'd visited her," Eileen retorted smoothly.

Angela must have caught the astonished look on Bryce's face because she smiled and said to him, "Judy and Bean are Eileen's and Max's cats."

"Our babies." Eileen corrected her, looking at Bryce for the first time. Her eyes widened and she shot Angela a look that Bryce couldn't fathom. "The King of Pentacles!"

"Forget it," Angela replied tersely and turned back toward their table.

"Now don't be stubborn," Eileen told her, following her over to the table and gazing with great interest at Bryce.

Bryce rose politely at her arrival, and Angela introduced them. Bryce noticed that Angela had a rather mulish set to her mouth. He wondered what on earth Eileen was talking about.

"Black hair," Eileen said significantly to Angela.

"He has gray eyes," Angela countered, leaving Bryce bewildered.

"I beg your pardon?"

"Never mind," Angela told him. "It's *not* important."

"Don't be silly. Of course it is." Eileen reached out to shake Bryce's hand. "I'm so glad Angie brought you to see us."

"Thank you."

"I'll fix you two something special," she said, her dark eyes twinkling. "You all just ignore the menu. It's so nice when Angela brings a—new person over here."

"You sound as if you're my mother," Angela said irritably.

"Well, why not? Someone's got to take care of you. Otherwise you'd spend your entire life with your head in the clouds, dreaming up stories and never taking a look at what's going on around you." She turned back to Bryce, saying brightly, "And what's your line of business, Bryce?"

"Give it up, Eileen," Angela said cryptically. "Bryce is a friend of my parents, and he's here to help me with a tax problem."

"Oh." Eileen's face fell. "You think that's what the cards meant? That the King of Pentacles was going to be someone you were working with?"

"Probably. If they meant anything—I don't think Gloria's the greatest with the tarot."

Eileen shrugged and said in a confidential tone to Bryce, "Angela's much more into palm reading. She doesn't think the cards are reliable."

"I'm right," Angela said. "It depends on who's doing the reading."

Bryce watched them, feeling rather like Alice at the Mad Hatter's tea party. Angela glanced at him and, seeing the wary look on his face, began to smile.

"We better stop," she told Eileen. "Bryce is beginning to think we're insane."

He started to make a polite demurral, but Eileen just chuckled, obviously unoffended.

"That's okay, so does Max. He's all into alternative health and natural foods, but somehow he can't see that there are other forces in the world beyond the rational and the tangible." She shrugged. "Maybe it's something about men. Left brain thinking."

"Probably," Angela agreed, casting a teasing grin in Bryce's direction.

When Eileen left them, Bryce turned to Angela. "Palmistry, huh? I guess I should have figured."

"Hush. You make it sound like some Gypsy fortune-teller thing."

"Isn't it?"

"I regard it as more of a science, really. There's quite a bit you can tell about a person by the lines and marks on their hands. You trust fingerprinting, don't you?"

"For identification, yes. I don't believe that you can look at a person's fingerprints, though, and tell whether he's a thief."

"I didn't say you could, but the lines on your fingers and in your hands are unique to you, and they tell a lot about you, too."

"Indeed." Bryce held out his hand, palm up. "Tell me about my hand, then."

Angela was a little startled by his willingness to engage in something as "off the beaten path" as palm reading, but she reached over and took his hand in her left hand and bent over the table to peer at it. Bryce noticed how warm and soft her hand was against his skin, smaller than his own hand and gentle in a way that made him feel strangely protective. Bryce liked the touch of her palm, but he ignored it resolutely.

"Well, in general you have the long hand that indicates an air or mental type—a thinker. But your palms are a little more rounded and your lines are deeper, more what people call an action hand or a fire type. So I'd say the two are combined. A thinker, but one who's also a doer. You see where your fingers are connected to your palm? That's your finger cast-off. If you ran a line across there, yours would be straight. That's a strong, even base, you see, so that indicates you have drive and self-confidence, assurance—even aggressiveness. And your thumb, well, your thumb indicates that you are an independent sort. See how low it's set on the hand. Also, it's long, which supports the cast-off of the fingers—it says you're tenacious and work hard to achieve your goals." She looked up at him. "How am I doing so far?"

He smiled. "I sound great. But, after all, you know me. You're aware that I own my own business, which would indicate drive and hard work, etc. You could probably tell me those things without even looking at my hand."

Angela quirked one eyebrow disapprovingly. "Skeptics always have another answer for anything you show them."

"Maybe that's because there is one."

She looked back down at his hand. "Here is your life line. Quite long and steady, although there are some little lines shooting off here at the beginning, and an island, too, indicating, I would think, problems when you were younger." She looked up quizzically. "In your childhood, perhaps?"

Bryce shrugged, his face unreadable. "Go on."

"Well, your head line is also strong and firm, going straight across your palm." She drew a finger along the middle line of his hand, and the movement sent a shock of pleasure running through Bryce, startling in its intensity.

He looked up at Angela's face, searching for some indication that she had felt the same electric sensation. But Angela was going calmly on. "This indicates clear, logical thought, but also a lack of imagination." She held up her own hand, pointing to the middle line of the three major ones. "See how mine curves downward...that indicates imagination.''

"That's something even I knew about you," he said pointedly.

"Well, here's something that surprises me, at least," she told him. "You have a well-developed mound of Venus." She stroked her thumb across the fleshy pad at the base of his thumb. "That's indicative of a passionate nature."

She looked up at him, and their gazes clung for a moment. Unconsciously she rubbed her thumb across the mound, and fire shot through Bryce at her touch. His mind went to the other night in his hotel room and the way she had melted at his kiss, suddenly hot and pliable in his arms. His breath grew a trifle uneven at the memory. He could see in Angela's eyes that she was remembering the moment, too. An impulse to kiss her seized him. He wondered what she would do. His hand turned, taking hers. He leaned forward across the table.

Five

Unconsciously Angela started to lean toward Bryce. Then she realized what she was doing, and she jerked her hand away, blushing. She could not imagine why she had acted the way she did. She was too honest to pretend to herself that there had been nothing sexually teasing in her touch. She didn't know why heat had risen in her when she took Bryce's hand or why she had felt impelled to stroke his palm. But she had seen the reaction in his eyes, had felt it in herself, and she knew that she was playing with fire. The other night should have taught her something, she knew; she was not naive or stupid. She had invited Bryce to dinner because of the upwelling of guilt and embarrassment in her for the way she had treated him when she was younger, not for any ulterior sexual motive. *Surely not.* Her motives had been perfectly innocent, even when she picked up his hand to read. *Hadn't they?*

She wondered what Bryce thought of her. She had sensed that he had been about to kiss her. She supposed she could not blame him if he had thought that she wanted him to. Perhaps he had even assumed that that had been the reason for her invitation. She sneaked a look at him.

He didn't appear angry. He had drawn back and was watching her without expression. Perhaps she was wrong and he had not meant to kiss her at all.

"I'm sorry," she said awkwardly. "I'm sure you must think it's foolish. It's just something fun to do at parties and things, anyway."

"Of course."

Angela felt terribly self-conscious. She looked down at her hands and searched her mind for something to talk about, something that had absolutely nothing to do with sex.

Finally Bryce spoke, and she sagged a little with relief. "Tell me something."

"All right."

"Precisely why did you see fit to play those jokes on me fifteen years ago?"

"Oh." Angela could feel the heat of embarrassment rising in her face again. This was not a subject she relished talking about, either. "Well..." She drew a deep breath and let it out. "Frankly, I resented you."

Bryce's eyebrows shot up. "What? Are you joking?"

"No. Why would I?"

"But why would you have resented me? You had everything. A beautiful home, great parents, money, looks."

"Looks!" Angela chuckled. "I wore braces and had wild red hair that stuck out in all directions and I was chubby."

"The potential was there—the smile, the eyes."

"Perhaps. But I definitely felt like a perfect mess." She shrugged. "I resented you because my parents liked you. You were like them. You understood them, and they understood you. I was such a disappointment to them, and I knew it. I couldn't be like them, and yet I felt so bad and guilty because I couldn't. So I took my feelings out on you. That's why I tormented you."

Bryce stared at her blankly. "Why? I don't understand. You weren't a disappointment to your parents. How could you have thought they liked me better than you? You're their daughter. They love you."

"Oh, I know they love me," Angela said with a grimace. "And we get along pretty well now, since I've made a success of my business and I can talk to them about things like profit margins and sales figures and all. But I was never like them. I think my mother looked at me the same way that mother duck must have looked at the ugly duckling—where did this kid come from? How can she be mine? What am I going to do with her?"

Bryce smiled fractionally. "I think all parents feel that way sometimes."

"Not sometimes. Always. I was a changeling in that family. My sister was just like Mom and Dad. She learned numbers almost as soon as she learned words. I don't mean just knew the names of the numbers...she understood the concept. She could do addition and subtraction before she started school. *I* was never even in the advanced math class. Jenny was the model student. She listened in class, did her homework, finished her tests before anyone else. I was a straggler, a daydreamer, a talker. All I was really interested in was recess and summer.''

Bryce chuckled. ''Your daydreaming paid off well for you.''

''I know. I can look back on it and see that, but it doesn't change how I felt at the time. Stupid and weird, a cuckoo in the nest.''

''And you felt I was trying to take your place.''

Angela nodded. ''It was childish. But there you were, talking their language, understanding them, *shining* for them. And there I was, the kid who never thought in clear, straight lines, who never came up with the practical solution to anything. I was the kind who'd make up these crazy, convoluted inventions that would take twice as long to do something than if you just did it normally.''

''I wasn't really trying to take your place, you know,'' Bryce said softly when she paused. ''I was just trying to make one of my own.''

''It *is* childish to continue holding a grudge.'' Angela smiled at him. Strangely enough, she felt something almost like friendship toward Bryce at the moment. Even though they had been on opposite sides of it, they had shared an experience. And he was being very understanding, even compassionate, about it, something she never would have dreamed of the man who had always seemed to her to have the emotions of a rock.

She stuck out her hand toward him. ''Shall we forgive and forget?''

''Kiss and make up?'' he agreed, smiling and reaching out to shake her hand.

The sexual connotation of his words struck them both, and the moment turned awkward again. Bryce's eyes went involuntarily to Angela's mouth. Their hands dropped to their sides without ever touching. Bryce cleared his throat and looked away.

Fortunately their food came soon, and they were able to bridge the uncomfortable moment by starting on their dishes. Eileen had outdone herself. She sent out first an appetizer of stuffed mushrooms, followed by a salad of all the latest trendy greens and, finally, the main course of pasta and vegetables tossed with a tangy, zesty sauce. It was accompanied by a loaf of hot whole wheat bread and a pot of sweet homemade butter.

After Bryce's first tentative bite, his eyebrows rose in appreciative surprise. "Why, this is delicious!"

"What did you think?" Angela asked indignantly. "That I'd take you someplace with bad food?"

"No. I just—well, I never imagined a vegetarian dish could taste this good."

Angela made a face at him. "Philistine."

"Sorry. I suppose I am." He smoothed the pale butter over the dark bread and took a bite. "Mmm. But you and Eileen have made a believer of me. I think the bread is even better than the pasta. What do you call this dish, anyway?"

"I don't know. I imagine it's one of Eileen's spur-of-the-moment concoctions. Maybe she'll name it Bryce's Rotini after you."

"Or perhaps the King of Pentacles' Rotini."

Angela chuckled. "Could be."

It was strange, she thought, but she was actually enjoying Bryce Richards's company. Perhaps he wasn't so bad, after all. Maybe all these years she had let her own insecurity influence her against him. Maybe one could be a number-juggler and still be all right. After all, her sister, Jenny, was a fun person once you got her off mathematical equations.

"Tell me something," she said, leaning forward. "What do you like to do? In your spare time, I mean."

Bryce looked at her as if she had spoken in a foreign language. "What do you mean?"

"I mean your spare time. Your activities. Hobbies. Whatever."

"Oh. Well, actually, the last few years I haven't had a lot of spare time. I've been busy getting the business off the ground."

"And now? I presume it's flying now."

"Yes. But I still work a lot."

"So all you do is work?"

"No." Bryce looked offended. "I, uh, I go to dinners, parties, things like that."

"With clients?"

"Yes."

"That doesn't count. Something you do for fun."

"I work out sometimes at the club. And I run."

Angela rolled her eyes expressively.

"The opera." Bryce looked pleased with himself. "I went to the opera two weeks ago."

"Did you enjoy it?"

"Of course. It was very..." He paused for a long moment, then grinned. "Boring, actually. I would have fallen asleep if they hadn't been singing so loud."

Angela chuckled.

"But I'm not completely inert socially," he protested. "I do date. I've been to movies and...that sort of thing."

"What was the last movie you saw?"

"Uh, actually, I—"

"That's what I thought. You need to loosen up. All work and no play and all that stuff."

He smiled faintly. "I'm afraid I'm not the type."

"To enjoy himself? Nonsense. Everyone should have something fun to do, an avocation that takes them away from work. Something light, with no redeeming value. That's what keeps you young and healthy."

"I thought it was food like this that did that."

"That, too. But you have to nourish your spirit, as well. Did you know that laughter actually induces healthy responses in your body?" She brightened. "Hey! Why don't we go to a club? There's a nice jazz bar not too far from here."

"I have work to do," Bryce replied automatically.

Angela grimaced. "It's Friday night. And it's almost ten o'clock. Nobody stays in their office till ten on a Friday."

"They do when they have a client who's in severe trouble."

"For Heaven's sake." Angela waved away his remark. "Your client releases you from your obligation tonight. Trust me, the problem will still be there tomorrow."

"That kind of attitude is what's gotten you into trouble."

"Don't be such an old poop. Come on, I insist." Angela jumped up and reached over to take his hand and pull him out of his chair.

Bryce found he couldn't keep from smiling back at Angela and standing up. He supposed he should insist on returning to the office and getting the work done, but he found himself reluctant to bring the evening to a close. He didn't really want to return to the office and work by himself. Besides, there was something very pleasant—more than pleasant, actually—about having her hand in his, pulling him along.

They walked through the empty restaurant to the front counter, where Eileen, through with her job, was sitting with Max, chatting. She turned and smiled expansively. "Did you enjoy your meal?"

"It was wonderful." Angela rhapsodized about the food for a few minutes while Eileen and Max beamed. "You're absolutely the best."

There was a small argument over who would pay their bill as both Bryce and Angela pulled out their credit cards. Eventually Angela won, insisting that she had asked him to come and that she had the better business excuse to take it off her taxes.

"You should understand that," she told him dryly.

"I do. I'm glad you remember to take the deductions."

"Honestly, Bryce, I'm not an idiot." Angela glared at him.

He grinned. "Just teasing."

"Isn't she sweet?" Eileen said to Bryce while Angela was busy paying the check.

Angela, listening to her, chuckled. "Don't try to get that past Bryce. He knew me when I was twelve. I used to play mean tricks on him."

"That doesn't count. All teenage girls play mean tricks, especially on boys."

"Especially Angela," Bryce added.

Angela responded with a grimace.

Undeterred, Eileen went on, "We never would have made it without Angie, you know."

"No, I didn't know that."

Eileen nodded emphatically. "It's true. We started on a shoestring. I mean, 'undercapitalized' doesn't even begin to describe it. Angela was just one of our customers, but when she heard that we were about to go under, she gave us the money we needed to set the restaurant up right. And not a word about income projections and security and all that stuff like the banks that turned us down."

Angela laughed. "Don't tell Bryce that. He'll be on my case for such poor business practices."

"Don't be silly. I'm sure he understands the difference between a warm heart and stupidity."

"Why, thank you." Bryce nodded gravely at Eileen and shot Angela a so-there look.

"Anyway," Angela went on, "it wasn't just kindness. I'd eaten here, remember. I knew how well your business would do if it was given the chance to get off the ground."

"Maybe so, but you were the only one willing to give us the chance." Eileen beamed at Angela.

Angela gave her friend a hug, promising to call her soon, and they left. The night was balmy and they strolled in a leisurely manner to Angela's car. It wasn't until they reached the car and separated that Bryce realized that he had been holding Angela's hand. A little unsettled, he slid into the low seat of the sports car and looked across at Angela. Somehow or other, around Angela he didn't quite act like himself, and that bothered Bryce.

He didn't like things that were unpredictable, and he knew that there was little predictability about Angela. He ought to avoid her like the plague. He should go back to the office right away, whether he actually did any work or not. Yet he found himself not saying a word as Angela pulled out into the street and headed away from the office.

Angela zoomed up to the first traffic signal and stopped. As they sat waiting for the light to change, she casually picked up the credit card receipt from the restaurant, which was sitting on top of her purse and stuck it into a pocket in the car door.

Bryce's brow went up. "That's where you put your business entertainment receipts?"

She nodded, then turned to look at him. "Why?" A tiny smile began to play on her lips. "I suppose you keep yours in a more orderly manner?"

"Of course," Bryce replied as the light changed and Angela started driving again. "You should jot it down, along with the reason for the dinner. A small notebook is good for that, and you can keep it in the glove compartment of your car, or in your purse or briefcase. Stick the receipt in the back of the notebook, and take it out the next day at the office and put it in its file."

Angela burst out laughing. "Oh, Bryce. I bet you keep your socks neatly rolled and lined up by color in your dresser drawer." She laughed even harder when she saw his expression. "God, I was right, wasn't I?"

"Close," he admitted, then added in a goaded voice, "What's wrong with a little order and precision? Why is it so good to be disorganized?"

"I don't know. I don't guess either one is good or bad. But I can't see living that way. Don't you get bored?"

"I don't spend a lot of time looking into my sock drawer, so I don't get bored by their order, no. In fact, I think that I would classify having to dig through my sock drawer every morning to find what I wanted to wear as boring.''

Angela cocked her head to one side, considering his words. "I never thought of it quite like that."

"Plus, I'm able to take all my entertainment expenses that way. I don't lose any."

"Neither do I." Angela pointed this out indignantly. "I always stick them right here, and every once in a while, I clean it out and take them up to Kelly."

Bryce stifled a groan.

"What's the matter with that? I don't lose them, and I don't have to waste that time writing them down. Kelly knows a lot more about it than I do."

"Do all your employees use this sort of accounting method?"

"I don't know. You'd have to ask Kelly." She looked at him suspiciously. "Why? Are you going to start making us fill out forms about our expenses?"

"It would probably help."

"Bryce! I don't want to have to do that. And I'm sure the people who work for us don't want to, either. Besides, only the sales force and Tim and I ever have entertainment write-offs. It's not that common. Oh, now look!" she exclaimed in exasperation. "I've missed the street where I meant to turn."

She made a sharp right turn at the next corner and circled the block to pull into a parking lot beside a small, drab brick building. She turned and looked at him sternly. "No more business talk. People come here to have fun, not talk about receipts and write-offs and all that. Okay?"

"Okay," he agreed, an amused smile playing on his lips. Looking at her, he found he had no desire to talk about anything regarding business.

"Good." Angela turned back and began to fluff and tweak her thick hair into place, using the rear-view mirror.

Bryce gazed at her idly, wondering how there could be something so alluring, so intimate and exciting about watching her perform such a simple task. When they got out of the car, Angela turned and looked at him critically, then insisted that he remove his suit coat and tie and leave them in the car.

"There," she said, unbuttoning the top button of his shirt and his cuffs and rolling his sleeves up, "that looks much better."

Taking his hand, Angela led him across the lot and into the old building. The entryway was dim, but Angela went confidently up the creaking wooden steps against the wall. The wail of a blues guitar grew louder as they moved upward, and at the top of the stairs, they stepped into a dark, cramped bar. A musician sat on a stool on a minuscule stage at the far end of the room, and there were more tables and chairs crammed into the rest of the room than Bryce would have thought possible. He suspected that the club was breaking a fire ordinance, but he kept his mouth shut, knowing how Angela would react to his saying something like that.

They made their way to an empty table against the back wall and sat down. The music was low and easy to listen to, and in between sets, Angela and Bryce talked.

Bryce had never been one who talked easily with people. He had always had the vaguely uneasy feeling that he was different, that others found him stiff and the things he talked about incomprehensible and boring. He rarely loosened up and talked freely except when he was with people like Angela's parents, who were interested in numbers. Even then, he felt limited to talking only about his job.

With Angela, who talked freely about any and everything, from songs to politics, it was somehow easy to talk. Bryce found himself joining in, laughing at her comments and adding his own, discussing their tastes in music and art—and, amazingly, finding them not that dissimilar. By the time the evening wound down, he was regaling her with some of his more interesting cases, and Angela was listening with gratifyingly wide-eyed amazement.

They didn't leave until the jazz bar closed, and their steps as they walked away from the small place were slow. Bryce took Angela's hand, and she leaned against his arm as they strolled along. Bryce could feel the heat of her body through his shirt, and below the rolled-up sleeves, where his bare skin touched hers, tantalizing frissons of pleasure snaked up his arm and down through his torso. He was aware of the faint scent of her perfume, warmed by her body, and of the nearness of her breasts and hips. He remembered how they had felt pressed against him the night he had kissed her. He remembered how swiftly his blood had turned to fire, how much he had wanted to tumble back onto his bed with her and explore every inch of her body.

What was it about her that made her so damn desirable? Even now, just the memory was making him hard and aching. She teased his senses, even though he could not accuse her of trying to. She simply aroused him, and he knew that he had felt it all evening long in subtle ways. Now, however, in the darkness with her body close to his, all subtlety was giving way to a building, throbbing need.

He glanced down at her face, sleepy and vague in the wash of moonlight, and wondered what she would think if he stopped and kissed her right here on the sidewalk. Would she stiffen, the mood broken, and pull away from him...or would she melt into his arms like thick, warm honey? His breath caught in his throat at the thought of it.

Bryce told himself it was foolish to think this way. For all that Angela had joked and talked with him tonight, she would not be interested in him, not in that way. She had been trying to make up to him for all the times she had played tricks on him as a teenager. She was assuaging her guilt, not looking for a man. For all he knew, she was already involved with someone, and even if she were not, Bryce was sure that he was not the sort of man she would choose. He was too staid, too dull, too practical. His world was bound by logic and numbers, and hers seemed to have no boundaries at all. The other night when they had kissed and she had seemed as caught up in the fire as he—surely that had been a fluke, a mere chance.

And if, by chance, she should respond to him, where would it lead? Bryce knew that any thought of a future was pointless. They were too different. *Hell, they even lived in different cities!* They would be bored within hours once they had made love. Or, worse, they would grow restless and irritated with each other. There could be nothing between them but a mere dalliance, and Bryce would never think of engaging in a fling with the daughter of people whom he respected and liked as much as he did Angela's parents. No. It was entirely out of the question.

Yet, looking at her, feeling her satiny flesh against his arm, tantalized by her scent, Bryce found it strangely difficult to hold onto his reasoned arguments. All the way back to the office, potently erotic images kept flickering in Bryce's mind. He couldn't stop imagining how Angela looked without her clothes on or how her skin would feel beneath the stroke of his hand. He thought of her breasts and thighs and had to bite down hard on his lip to pull his mind away from the arousing thoughts before his desire became all too evident.

Angela stopped her car in front of the office, right behind Bryce's large dark Mercedes. She put the car into Park and turned toward him. Bryce gazed back at her for a long moment. He wanted to lean over and press his lips to hers. The car was small, and the space that separated them was narrow. It would be so easy to touch her. He could smell the faint scent of her perfume in the air. Her mouth was soft and moist, her lips slightly parted. Bryce swallowed as the flames in his abdomen licked higher.

"Well, uh . . ." His voice came out hoarse, and he cleared it nervously. "Thank you for the dinner and the evening."

"You're welcome."

"I'd better go now. It's late."

Angela nodded. Her eyes were immense and velvety in the darkness. He wondered what she was thinking. For a moment the two of them were perfectly still. Every nerve in Bryce's body was taut. Abruptly he turned away and opened his door.

"Good night." He swung out of the door and closed it.

"Wait!" Angela opened her door and jumped out.

Bryce stopped and turned to look at her. "What?"

Angela's mind was blank for a moment. She didn't know why she had jumped out—except that she had thought he was going to kiss her and then he didn't and she wished that he had. But she could hardly tell him that.

"Uh—well, I was going to say, maybe you'd like to come to Tim's costume party next Friday night. I thought maybe you'd like to come with me."

Bryce was aware of a strong urge to accept her invitation. "Thank you, but I don't think so. I'm not much for costume parties. Besides, it isn't even Halloween. It's April."

"It doesn't have to be Halloween for a costume party. Raleighites love costumes. And Tim's are something special. You shouldn't miss a chance to see it. You have to park down at the foot of the driveway and they take you up to the house and—well, you'll see. It's fun, getting to dress up and pretend to be something you're not."

"I was never very good at pretending," Bryce told her with a wry smile.

"Oh, come on. There's got to be a streak of the romantic in you. Why else did you choose the occupation you did? It may be numbers, but it's not plain accounting. Doing security and investigations for corporations has got a certain touch of derring-do about it, don't you think? Sort of accountant-cum-secret agent?"

Bryce chuckled at that description of his job. *Trust Angela Hewitt to imbue his work with mystery and daring. She couldn't accept anything as dull as the plain truth.*

"You're incorrigible," he told her. "I think you're applying *your* imagination to my job. What I do are things that most people would find deadly dull."

Angela shrugged. "Say what you like. But, personally, I think you're suppressing your sense of fun. Just try coming to the party, and you'll enjoy it. Didn't you have fun tonight?"

"Well, yes, I did, but that's not the same as making a fool of myself in some costume."

"You won't make a fool of yourself," Angela said in exasperation. "Everyone there will be in costume. Say, you could come as a white knight. You know, slaying the dragon of the IRS."

"I'm hardly a white knight, I'm afraid." But Bryce couldn't help but smile back at her.

"Well, perhaps the cavalry, then. They were always coming in the nick of time in the old Westerns, weren't they?"

He shook his head, though the traces of a grin still clung to his chiseled lips. "Give it up, Angela. I'm a lost cause. Not the costume party type."

"Sure you are. Everybody is. It's like being a kid again. Don't you remember how much fun it was when you were little? On Halloween, when you'd dress up in a costume and trek around the neighborhood, pretending to be spooky, but in reality being too scared to even go up to that one dark house on the block that everybody always avoided?"

"I never had a costume. I didn't do Halloween."

Angela stared at him in amazement. "You're not serious."

"Have you ever known me to be anything else?"

"Well, no, actually, but—no costumes! No Halloween! Not even when you were real little?"

"Not even then," he replied shortly. "Look. My mother wasn't the kind who sewed costumes. And I never saw the sense in wasting the money. Besides, where we lived there was more than one house where you wouldn't want to ring the doorbell. Now, I really must go."

Angela could think of nothing to say. She was stunned by Bryce's words. But as she turned away, her mind was already busily scheming about some way to get Bryce Richards to his first costume party.

Six

Angela was disappointed. She had been sure that Bryce was going to kiss her when she pulled up in front of the office, but then he had pulled back at the last moment and gotten out of her car. It wasn't that she had planned for the kiss to happen or that she had spent the evening trying to entice him into it. She had simply acted on the spur-of-the-moment in inviting Bryce to dinner and then again when she badgered him into going out on the town with her. But as the evening progressed, she had become more and more aware of the way he looked at her, and she had thought that he wanted to kiss her.

She had also been growing more and more aware of *him* during the evening: the movement of his hands as he talked; the way he shrugged out of his suit jacket, the muscles of his chest flexing beneath the plain white shirt; the odd silver-gray color of his eyes beneath the straight black brows; the firmness of his mouth. Especially his mouth. Her eyes had been drawn back to his lips time and again as they talked. There was something very intriguing to her about the curve of his lower lip, fuller and more sensuous than the upper one. She kept remembering the way his lips had felt against hers, hot and demanding, and she had anticipated his kiss.

Then it hadn't happened.

That was all right, of course. It wasn't as if she wanted anything to happen between them—because she didn't. Nor was she really attracted to him—or, at least, only a little bit. But she would have liked to discover if the other night in his room had been a momentary aberration or if Bryce Richards's kisses actually did have an incredible power. Angela freely admitted that she was incorrigibly curious, and Bryce had definitely sparked her curiosity. He seemed so staid, so dull, and yet...the passion she had felt in his arms the other night had been anything but staid and dull. And she had found him interesting to talk to when they went out, even fun. They had laughed and talked like friends, not like two people with nothing in common. The more fun they had had, the more she had thought about those kisses in his hotel room, and the more she had wondered.

Angela was restless all weekend, and she thought up a hundred excuses to go to the office, but she restrained herself. She had no real reason to go; she could work on her game ideas just as well at home, and that was the only thing she needed to do. She refused to allow herself to hang around the office waiting for a chance to see Bryce or to talk to him, like a junior high schoolgirl loitering in the halls in the hopes of a glimpse of some football hero.

She tried to get involved in a half-dozen projects, including her new game, but nothing held her interest for long. She played a few games; she went next door to visit Jim and Harbaugh, but neither was at home. She paced through her apartment, trying to think of a way to lure Bryce to Tim's charity ball, then telling herself that she was silly to even worry about it.

She half expected the phone to ring all weekend, though she told herself that she did not change her mind about going to the lake house in the hopes that Bryce would call her. However, her phone did not ring—or, rather, the three times that it did, it was not Bryce on the other end of the line. Once it was her mother calling from Charlotte.

"Oh, hi, Mother." Angela sat down with a sigh, feeling deflated and not wanting to admit it. "How are you?"

"Fine, dear," her mother's well-modulated voice came across the wires. "And you?"

"Getting by. I guess you know about Bryce coming down."

"Yes, and I was so happy to hear that you were going to let him help you. You know, everyone can use a little help now and then."

"I know. It wasn't that I didn't want to accept help. It was just..."

"I know, you didn't want to accept help from him. I still fail to understand why you find him so objectionable. Bryce is a very admirable young man. He's made quite a success of himself, and he's very intelligent. Well-spoken. Good-looking."

"Yes, Mom, I know. He's a paragon among men."
Angela remembered suddenly why she had so thoroughly disliked Bryce Richards.

"That's exactly what I mean—that tone when you talk about him. The air of sarcasm. It isn't at all logical, you know, given the excellent qualities he has."

"I know, I know," Angela interjected irritably. "But the fact is, logic doesn't have much to do with how you feel about another person. I mean, did you *logically* fall in love with Dad? Did you sit down and draw up a sensible list, itemizing his good points and his bad points, then decide that you loved him?"

"Of course not. Although, certainly, I was aware of his excellent qualities, and they were a large part of why I fell in love with him. Anyway, who's talking about love? I'm just asking you to be nice to Bryce, not marry him." She paused, and tension sizzled in the silence. Finally Marina Hewitt went on cautiously, "What is it exactly you're talking about?"

"Just friendship," Angela said hastily. "That's all. Actually, Bryce has turned out not to be so bad. I must have matured."

"I'm stunned. No whoopee cushions on his chair seat?"

"No. Nor any plastic bugs in his salad. And, unfortunately, I couldn't get into his room at the Radisson to wind string all over it."

"Oh, Lord, I'd forgotten that. That time we took him with us to the beach. I was mortified."

"It was quite a project. Almost a work of art."

"I considered strangling you."

Angela chuckled. "You know, Bryce really was remarkably patient."

"He was a saint. It wouldn't have been so bad if it hadn't been for his background."

"His background?" Angela's smile fell from her face. "What do you mean?"

"You know, his mother and all that. He wanted very much to be accepted."

"What are you talking about? What about his mother?"

"I forgot you didn't know about it. Well, it's not really my story to discuss."

"Mother! You can't leave me hanging like this!"

"It's his private matter. I won't gossip. Don't you go asking him, either. It'll just call up old wounds that are better forgotten. Suffice it to say that he had a difficult childhood—poverty, neglect. He was on scholarship at the university, and such a complex, silent, intelligent young man. You could see the brilliance shining in him, but he had trouble relating to people. That's why I more or less took him under my wing."

Angela plopped down on the stool by the phone, stunned. "I—I didn't know."

"Of course not, dear. You were only twelve at the time, after all, and it wouldn't have been appropriate to tell you about it. Besides, as I said, it's not really my story to tell."

Angela twisted the telephone cord around her finger, guilt gnawing at her. "I wouldn't have been so mean to him. I mean, I never guessed that he had any problems."

"Teenagers tend to be that way."

"Now I feel even worse." Angela thought of the thin, dark, impassive boy whom she had disliked so thoroughly. All that time, when she had thought him icy and unfeeling, a robot trying to steal her place in her family, had he really been a lonely, deprived boy? Had he been struggling to find his place in the world, hurt by a painful childhood? Her eyes felt suddenly hot, as if she were about to cry.

"Don't worry about it. It's in the past now," her mother told her practically. "Anyway, I'm not sure your jokes weren't for the best. Bryce had such a chip on his shoulder back then. He hated for anyone to lend him a helping hand. He was suspicious that people were nice to him because they pitied him. I think perhaps he didn't feel that in our house, partly because you were so relentlessly adolescent and hostile. It reassured him in an odd way."

Angela groaned. "That's not exactly comforting."

She could almost see her mother's shrug on the other end of the line. Comfort was not one of Marina's main concerns. She preferred the facts.

"I'm surprised he agreed to come help us," Angela went on. "I must be his least favorite person."

"I applied a little emotional pressure," Marina replied candidly. "I could hardly let you get into trouble with the IRS, could I?"

"Are you sure Bryce can help me?"

"Of course. I don't worry about you now. Bryce is the best I know at things like this. He's not only mathematical, but he's also quite inventive and...oh, I don't know, almost *intuitive* about spotting problems."

There was a pause, then Angela said softly, "You think I'm an idiot, don't you?"

"Heavens, no, whatever gave you that idea?"

"For getting into this mess with the government."

"Lots of people get into trouble with the IRS, even those who are quite astute in money matters. And since I don't even know what the circumstances are, I can hardly judge whether you were foolish. I'm sure you aren't as careful as you should be about such things. You've always been a trifle..."

"Rash?" Angela supplied the word. "Careless?"

"I think impulsive was more the word I was looking for. And, yes, you can be careless about some things in a way that amazes me. But, dear, I hardly expect you to be like me. You are yourself, and everyone loves you just that way."

Angela felt slightly stunned. Apparently this was a day for surprises from her mother. "Really?"

"Goodness, yes. Angela, are you feeling all right? You seem a bit vague this afternoon."

"No. I'm fine. I'm simply amazed, I guess, at my own ignorance sometimes."

Her mother laughed lightly. "Well, welcome to the human race, dear."

Angela carefully avoided going in to work early Monday morning, just as she had kept herself away from the office all weekend. When she did get there, she went straight to her own office and sat down at her desk, but she was sure to leave the door to her office invitingly open. It was difficult to make herself work. The blue screen of her computer remained embarrassingly blank, and the yellow pad on the desk before her was covered with scribbles and drawings and not a single constructive idea.

She wondered where Bryce was—in Kelly's office or the general accounting room or perhaps holed up in some cubbyhole of his own, poring through books of green-barred computer printouts. Doubtless *he* wasn't having any problems concentrating on his work.

She was staring at her computer screen, mesmerized by the blinking cursor light, when a tap at her door brought her to with a start. Whirling her chair around to face the door, she cracked her shin against a drawer corner and let out a yelp. Rubbing her leg, she looked at the man standing in the doorway, a brown paper sack in his hand. It was Bryce, of course. She cursed under her breath as she offered him a bright smile.

"Hi. Sorry. I'm always knocking into things." She rose to her feet, motioning him to come in.

He closed the door and walked over to her desk. They stood for a moment, looking at each other awkwardly, the expanse of her desk between them. Bryce proffered the sack to her.

"Care for some lunch? It's hardly the quality of the other night's meal, but I thought we might, uh, share a sandwich and talk."

"Sure." Angela tried to quell the sudden, rapid beating of her heart inside her chest. "I didn't even realize it was lunchtime yet."

"It's only eleven-thirty. I eat early. I usually get to work a little after seven."

Angela made a face as she began to clear off space on her desk. "Needless to say, I don't get here that early. But since I didn't have any breakfast, I can probably eat."

She laid out the sandwiches, chips and drinks, talking in a fast, nervous way and all the while thinking that she was acting like an idiot. It wasn't as if she'd never been around Bryce. After all, they'd spent the whole evening together Friday, and she had talked and laughed with him like an old friend. Yet here she was acting as nervous as a schoolgirl on a first date. Somehow the intervening weekend—or perhaps it was the thoughts she'd been having over that time—had made her feel awkward with him.

"How have you been doing with the books?" she asked brightly, biting into the deli sandwich even though she suddenly felt not at all hungry.

Bryce shrugged. "I can see why the IRS is suspicious. Your sales were up quite a bit last year, yet your profits were down."

"Yes, but there's a reason for that. We tried to explain it to the IRS," Angela said, putting down her sandwich. "We hired two more people. They're involved in the CD-Rom games. It's a growing area for us. And we bought some equipment, a different software system for our shipping."

"Yeah, I know. Kelly told me. Still, there's something that feels hinky about the numbers."

"What do you mean?" Angela's brows knotted.

"I'm not sure. There's just something wrong. I haven't put my finger on it yet."

"You mean, like some kind of error that we're missing?"

Bryce shook his head. "I don't think so. Your numbers justify, and they shouldn't if there's an error. But the software system and the employees don't add up to enough to account for the drop."

"There are probably more expenses than those."

"I'll check through them all." He hesitated, then went on, "I'm sure what the Feds are thinking is that your company cooked up some of those expenses to cut down on taxes."

He looked at her. Angela gazed back at him blankly for a moment. Then she realized the question that was hovering behind his statement.

"Are you asking me if we did?" she asked, her temper rising.

"It's not unheard of. And if you did, you need to tell me. There's no point in my going through this if, in fact, you all have played with the figures. I doubt you'll be able to get it past the IRS agents."

"How can you think that?" Angela cried, jumping to her feet. "How can you believe that we would have cooked our books?"

His words cut her to the quick. She thought about the way she had been mooning over him all weekend, thinking that there was something brewing between them—*and all the while he'd been thinking that she was a crook!*

"Calm down. I didn't say you had," Bryce reminded her coolly. "I *asked* you. I want to make sure before I get any further into it."

"But to even ask implies that you think I'm capable of it."

"A lot of people don't regard an attempt to defraud the IRS in quite the same light as real thievery," Bryce explained wryly. "Most people spend their time trying to avoid paying more tax."

"Legally. But not by fraud. Not by making up a whole bunch of expenses that didn't exist." She stalked over to the window, then whirled and glared at him. "If nothing else, why would we be so stupid as to hire you to find what's wrong if we knew that it was because we'd cheated on our taxes? Why waste the money?"

"I don't know. Maybe to throw off suspicion. It's something that is possible." He stood up, his face lined with exasperation. "Stop reacting so emotionally. I didn't say you had done it. But I have to explore all the possibilities. I've found that it doesn't pay in this business to assume anything. Nor is it advisable to trust someone simply because you know them."

"Is that the way you live your life?" Angela asked, aghast. "Never trusting anyone? I'd hate to be you."

"Of course I trust certain people. Your parents, for instance. But I don't jump in right away with my trust. I have to know a person well. I take my time and make sure that they're worthy of trust."

"But sometimes . . . can't you just tell? Don't you ever simply feel that this person or that is good or special? Don't you ever like someone for no reason?"

"Sometimes," he replied noncommittally. "But I don't *count* on it until I know them a lot better."

Angela groaned and plopped back down into her chair. "Honestly, Bryce, you're so . . . *practical!*"

A faint smile curved his lips. "Not everyone would consider that a terrible feature."

"It's not terrible. It's just that you're so different from me." There was a curiously forlorn feeling inside her as she said the words. All the thoughts she'd been having about Bryce this weekend had been foolish daydreaming. A relationship was out of the question. They could never get along. No doubt Bryce had been logical enough to figure that out; she was sure *he* hadn't spent the past two days mooning over her. He, of course, had been down here at the office working.

"Well, we did not doctor our books." Angela went on flatly. "We didn't make up any expenses in order to save ourselves taxes. Does that satisfy you?"

"Yes. I'm glad."

Angela picked her sandwich back up and bit into it, feeling rather disgruntled, and for a long time there was nothing but silence in the room.

"I, uh, wanted to thank you for the other night," Bryce said finally. "It was very nice."

"Good. I'm glad you enjoyed it." Angela kept her voice light and cool. She wasn't about to let him think that it had meant any more to her than a business entertainment, a little dinner and evening with her accountant.

"Don't be like this, Angela. I didn't really think that you were dishonest. But I would be remiss if I didn't explore every possibility."

"I'm aware of that. I just thought after we'd gone out the other night—oh, forget it."

"No. I won't." Bryce set down his food and shoved it aside. He leaned over the desk, fixing Angela with his gaze. "It's not something I'm likely to forget. I tried to all weekend, and it didn't work."

Angela felt suddenly as if there were a huge lump in her throat. She laid her sandwich aside. "What are you talking about?"

"You. Me. Last Friday night." Bryce got up and came around the desk, reaching down to grasp Angela's arms and pull her to her feet. "About the fact that I kept wanting to kiss you, and I didn't. I spent the past two days cursing myself for being such a fool."

"Did you?" Angela responded weakly. "So did I."

Bryce grinned as his mouth came down to fasten on hers.

He kissed her slowly, gently, not in a hard, passionate rush as he had the first time, but as if he had all the time in the world and wanted to explore every aspect of her. Finally, when Angela felt as if her knees might buckle at any second, he pulled his mouth from hers and began to press tiny kisses over her jaw and down her throat. Then, slowly, he brought his lips up the side of her neck, pausing here and there to taste her flesh.

Angela felt as if she were melting. His lips were velvety upon her skin and yet so hot she thought they must have seared her. "Bryce..."

"I like the way that sounds." Bryce brushed her thick hair back from her face, his hand sinking into the silken, curling mass, and kissed her ear.

A shaky moan emitted from Angela's lips. Bryce took her earlobe between his lips and nibbled at it, sending shivers of delight through her. Her abdomen blossomed with heat, and she sagged against him, not sure she could stand up without help.

His tongue was like liquid fire as it traced the convolutions of her ear, then returned to tease and caress her earlobe. Bryce put his hands on her shoulders and slowly slid them down over her back and onto her hips. His hands caressed the firm curve of her buttocks, squeezing and releasing. He drew in a sharp breath, and his mouth moved back to hers, seizing it in a long, demanding kiss. His tongue delved into her mouth; his lips moved hungrily against hers.

Angela trembled. Her whole body seemed to have burst into flames at his kiss, like dry tinder to a match. Bryce's hands slid over her hips and around to the sides, then moved back up, stopping only when he reached the undercurve of her breasts. His fingers burned through the cloth of her blouse, creating a tender ache in her breasts and loins. Slowly, still kissing her, Bryce cupped her breasts and moved his thumbs in lazy circles around her nipples, the circles growing ever smaller until it was only the small buds themselves that he touched. He took her nipples between his thumbs and forefingers, softly rolling and squeezing. Heat flooded between Angela's legs, throbbing and damp. It occurred to her that she was still fully dressed, as was he, yet he had made her so hungry and aching for him that she yearned to take him inside her right now.

"Oh, Angela!" Bryce pulled back, sucking in air. His face was flushed and heavy with sensuality, his lips slightly parted. His eyes were dark and hungry.

Angela gazed back at him, unable to speak, surging with wild sensations and confused emotions.

"This is insane," he breathed.

Angela nodded.

"We're in the office, and it's the middle of the day."

"I know." She smiled wryly, her sense of humor coming to her rescue, stiffening her trembling legs and allowing her to move away and sit down. "The door isn't even locked."

Bryce mumbled a short expletive and stalked away to the window. He stood for several minutes, staring out. Angela put her elbows on her desk and leaned her head on her hands, trying to recover her breath. Their first kiss that night in his room had not been an aberration, she realized, no matter how she had tried to convince herself that it was. In another moment, unlocked door or not, she would have been ready to slide to the floor and make love with him.

Thank God, she told herself, that Bryce had had enough presence of mind to stop. Her words echoed hollowly in her head. She knew, deep down, that they were a lie. She had not wanted him to stop at all.

"I want you," Bryce said baldly.

Angela didn't turn around. "But?"

"But what?"

"I don't know. That's what I'm asking—there was a 'but' in your voice."

"All right. But we can't rush into it. I—you're Marina's daughter."

"What does that have to do with it?" Angela whipped around, her eyes flashing. "I am myself, not someone's daughter, and it's me you're wanting to take to bed, so don't start bringing other people into it."

"I can't help it. Your parents are very special to me. I respect them."

"Oh, that's great," Angela retorted sarcastically. "Usually the issue is whether you'll respect *me* in the morning, not my parents."

"I would respect both of you," Bryce replied stiffly, frowning. "But you have to see that this complicates the issue."

"The *issue?*" Angela's voice rose to a squeak. "Now I'm an issue?"

"Dammit, Angela, stop trying to start an argument. Believe me, I would love to throw caution to the winds at the moment, but someone has to be sensible. We have to consider the consequences."

"*You* consider the consequences," Angela said rudely and swung back around to face her desk. "And do it somewhere else. I have work to do."

"Angela . . ."

"No. Go away." Angela felt treacherous tears rising in her, and she had to swallow hard to keep control of her voice. "Don't bother to tell me when you've resolved 'the issue.' I'm no longer interested."

She heard Bryce sigh. He came toward her and stopped behind her, but she refused to look up. Finally, with a low, inarticulate growl, Bryce walked around her and out the door.

Angela kicked the back panel of her desk. It hurt her toes, but it made her feel so much better that she kicked it two more times. She folded her arms on her desk and dropped her head to rest on them and sat for several minutes, wishing that Bryce Richards had never come to town.

Seven

Angela straightened and took a step back from the mirror. The stiff, wide farthingale beneath her skirt knocked over a small vase as she moved. Muttering an oath, Angela righted the bottle. Elizabethan dresses were romantic, but she was beginning to discover that they were completely impractical. When Kelly had shown her this dress last week, she had immediately decided she would wear it to Tim's costume party instead of the Maladora costume. Maladora might be sexy, but the slinky dress couldn't compare to the way this one made her waist look tiny or the way the stiff lace collar rising behind her head framed her face delicately. She had not given a thought to how difficult it was to wear.

Now she did. It had been a real struggle to get it on by herself, and it seemed as if everywhere she went the thick roll of material that made her skirts stand out

stiffly to either side of her hips knocked into things.
How had the women back then ever gotten around?
Also, the brocade dress, along with the petticoats and
farthingale, weighed her down, and the stiff collar,
braced against her shoulders, was making her back
ache.

Angela had considered not going to the party at all.
She didn't really want to. Ever since that scene with
Bryce in her office, she had not felt much in the party
mood. She had given up her idea of enticing Bryce into
going to the party with her, and without him, it had
lost much of its appeal. If it had been anyone but her
longtime partner giving the party, she was sure she
would have ducked out of it. But this was Tim's big
production every year, and he would be very hurt if
she didn't come. Besides, it would be decidedly un-
professional, since so many of the people they dealt
with in their business would be there.

Angela turned first to one side and then the other,
inspecting herself in the mirror. The heavy brocade
gown was ivory colored and shot through with gold
threads, subtly glittering. It was wasp-waisted in the
Elizabethan style with a stiffened bodice that pushed
her breasts up until they threatened to overflow the
square-cut neckline. A long rope of fake pearls was
twisted around her throat several times like a choker,
then fell in a long loop down to her skirts, as she had
seen once in a picture of Elizabeth I. A stiffened lace
collar rose from the neckline and up behind her head,
framing her face. The final touch was an ivory snood,
of the sort often worn by the doomed Mary, Queen of
Scots, upon her head. In the back her thick red hair
was gathered up into a golden net attached to the bottom of the cap, and in the front the snood came down

in a point in the middle, touching the center of her forehead. Pearls lined the edge of the heart-shaped, stiffened front.

It was the effect she had desired—more, really. She looked foreign, mysterious, romantic. She wondered what Bryce would have thought of it if he had seen her in the costume. It had been him she had thought of when she saw the dress and decided she wanted it instead of the Maladora costume. But then, after the way they had parted in her office, she didn't have the nerve to ask him again to go with her. Bryce might be attracted to her, but he did not want to be, and Angela was not about to make a fool of herself over him.

The doorbell rang, surprising Angela, and she sidled through the doorway, careful not to bump the farthingale into anything else. When she opened the door, she simply stood there for a moment, her jaw dropping open in shock. Bryce Richards stood before her.

But what a Bryce! It wasn't the man she knew, but a dark-haired, silver-eyed gambler. He was dressed in black, with a white shirt underneath; ruffles cascaded down the front of the shirt and flowed from his wrists. A black string tie was fastened around the collar, and a black felt hat was on his head. He held a long, very thin cigar in one hand.

"You look like you just stepped off a riverboat!" Angela exclaimed. "Or maybe out of *Gone With the Wind.*"

Bryce smiled. "That was the idea. Dorothy told me it was the perfect costume for me."

"Dorothy? Our receptionist?"

"Yes. I figured if she had made your costume, she must know something about them. So I asked her where to get one and what I should get. She thought a riverboat gambler would probably make me feel the least foolish. I guess she's right. I feel enough of an idiot like this—I hate to think what I'd feel like dressed up like a knight."

Angela smiled. She suspected that she was glowing. Bryce was going to Tim's party, and he was obviously here to take her to it.

Angela stepped back, and Bryce followed her into the condominium. His eyes ran down her figure appreciatively. "You've changed costume."

"Yeah. I decided that sexy Maladora stuff just wasn't me." Angela spread out her arms and turned around to show off the dress. "How do you like it?"

"You're—it's lovely." He looked a little stunned. His eyes dropped involuntarily to the tops of her creamy breasts, which looked in danger of popping out at any moment.

Angela smiled, pleased that she had made an impression. "Thank you."

He seemed unable to pull his eyes away from the white expanse of her chest revealed by the low, square-cut neckline. "Are you supposed to be Elizabeth I?"

Angela shrugged. "No, not especially. Just a generic Elizabethan lady."

"You don't look very generic. I'd say you look quite unique."

She narrowed her eyes suspiciously. "Is that a euphemism for 'strange'?"

A smile cracked his usually reserved face. "No. Not at all. A synonym for 'beautiful,' perhaps."

"Oh, my," Angela teased, "you're going to ruin your reputation as a dull C.P.A. if you keep making remarks like that." She paused for a moment, then

went on, "What made you change your mind—about
the party, I mean?"

"I'm not sure." His brows knit in a frown. "I think,
maybe, I got tired of being me."

Angela's eyebrows went up. "What does that
mean?"

"Sometimes it gets awfully dull being a stick-in-the-
mud."

Angela turned the full wattage of her smile on him.
"Well, I'm glad you decided to get out of the mud tonight."

Bryce hardly looked like anything dull tonight. He
looked hard, perhaps, maybe even a little dangerous,
but also dashing and handsome. And he was looking
at her in a way that made her feel warm and tingly all
over.

"You ready to go?" he asked.

"Yes. And you are definitely driving. I doubt very
seriously that this dress would fit behind a steering
wheel."

A faint smile warmed Bryce's lips as he stood aside
for her to pass in front of him. "I'd say only a carriage would do for that dress. Or perhaps a sedan
chair."

They stepped out the front door, and Angela locked
it behind them. "Oh," she said, glancing over at the
door next to her. "I forgot. I promised Jim I'd show
him my costume."

"Who?"

"My next-door neighbor. He loves stuff like this."
Angela turned, almost knocking a plant off its stand,
and went to the next door to knock.

Jim opened the door a moment later. "Oh, my," he said, his eyes widening. "Queen Elizabeth the First, as I live and breathe. Harbaugh, come look at our girl."

Harbaugh, taller and younger than Jim, with a muscular build and a serious face, appeared behind Jim in the doorway. He smiled. "You look like you stepped out of a history book."

"Thank you." Angela dipped them a little curtsey, then turned toward Bryce. "Jim, Harbaugh, I'd like for you to meet Bryce Richards."

Bryce came forward to shake hands. Jim's brows went up and he shot a knowing look toward Angela. Only two days ago Angela had been sitting glumly on his couch and telling him all about her and Bryce's abortive relationship.

"It's so nice to meet you," Jim said. "Wouldn't you two like to come in for a drink?"

"No, we'd better not," Angela demurred.

Jim leaned in, giving her a hug, and murmured, "Very nice. What happened?"

Angela chuckled and whispered back, "Tell you later."

"You better." Jim stepped back, his eyes twinkling. "You kids have fun."

Bryce drove quickly, competently, following Angela's directions to Tim's home in the rolling land north of Raleigh. They crossed the belt line and soon were on a winding road. Trees grew close to the road and whatever houses there were could not be seen.

They turned onto another narrower road and in a moment Angela said, "There it is, straight ahead. See the open gates? Oh, and look!"

Two large men dressed as Moorish warriors stood just inside the gates, and as Bryce's car turned into the driveway, they raised long spears, crossing them dramatically so that they blocked the driveway.

"Good Lord." Bryce stopped the car and shot a disbelieving look at Angela, but he pushed the button to open his window as one of the burly men came toward him, spear in hand.

"He wants this," Angela told Bryce and handed him the invitation. "People often try to crash Tim's parties because they're so famous. Besides, it adds a certain drama."

"I'll say," Bryce commented dryly, holding out the white square to the man.

The robed and turbaned warrior took the invitation and examined it. Angela, watching him, couldn't suppress a shiver. Even knowing, as she did, that he was a N.C. State football player dressed up in costume, there was something very foreign and menacing about the silent, impassive figure.

With a brusque nod, the guard handed back the invitation and pointed to an area to the left of the driveway, where many cars were already parked. "Leave your car there," he growled. "Then wait for Andre to drive you to the house."

Obediently Bryce pulled the car into the nearest available spot, and he and Angela waited beside the driveway. The two guards ignored them, standing stonily in the middle of the gates. The driveway climbed a rise and curved into the unknown, the rest of it blocked by trees and darkness. The pale light of a full moon flooded the landscape, lighting it yet leaving it mysteriously shadowed as well.

"Who's Andre?" Bryce leaned down and asked Angela in a stage whisper that seemed appropriate to the night and the locale.

Angela shrugged. "I don't know. But I suspect we'll know it when we see him."

Another car turned into the driveway and went through the same routine with the guard. They, too, parked their car and came over to join Bryce and Angela.

The man was dressed as a knight in a suit of silver plastic armor, and the woman was a Gypsy with wildly curling raven hair.

"Hey, Angela," a distinctive coastal North Carolina accent came out of the knight's headgear, and the man pushed up the visor with a clumsy, gloved hand to reveal the face of Stephen Jenesky, one of the brains of a local computer company. His face was flushed inside the hot suit, but he was grinning from ear to ear. Stephen was still a kid at heart; like Tim, his study at home was chock full of the latest in computer game gadgetry. He had a sound system attached to his computer that practically rattled the walls when he played a jet simulation game.

"Stephen! And Terri? Is that you?"

Terri giggled delightedly. "I told Stevie that this wig was almost as good a disguise as his helmet!"

Angela introduced the couple to Bryce. Then Bryce, who was standing facing Angela and gazing up the driveway, said dryly, "I believe I see Andre approaching."

The entire group turned to look. Coming toward them was an old-fashioned carriage. It was painted a shiny black, and a coat of arms was painted in gold on the door. A coachman in red livery and a white wig drove a team of four white horses, and beside him sat another liveried attendant.

"If that isn't just like Tim," Stephen commented admiringly. "Where do you suppose he found that?"

"If I know Tim, he's been searching for it ever since the last party."

"Isn't that the truth?" Terri agreed. "He always has to top himself."

The coach turned slowly behind the guards and came back to the group and stopped. The driver said nothing, just stared straight ahead of him. The footman, however, climbed down and came around to open the carriage door for them, bowing with a flourish.

Bryce helped Angela up into the carriage after the other couple, then climbed in beside her. "Tim believes in going all out, doesn't he?" he murmured into her ear.

Angela smiled. "Just wait. This is only the beginning."

The carriage lumbered off, starting up the incline and turning the curve. There, in the middle of the road, stood an enormously tall figure clad in a long dark blue robe decorated with glittering silver quarter moons and stars. A wizard's cap was on his head, making him loom even taller. From head to foot he looked to be at least eight feet tall.

All four of them stared, agog, out the window. The vision took two long strides forward and spread out his arms. The robe fell like bat wings from his arms, and he was a splendid, imposing picture.

"Who comes here?" His voice was impossibly deep and a little distorted, like a demon in a movie.

"He's wearing stilts," Bryce said thoughtfully. "And using one of those electronic devices that disguises your voice."

"No. Don't analyze it," Angela told him. "You'll ruin it. Just enjoy the experience."

"We are the Earl of Stansbury's men," the coach-man answered in an English accent. "And we come to bring his lordship's guests to the ball."

"Then you may pass," the figure said grudgingly. "But, remember that you pass through my enchanted woods as you ride to his castle. Sights such as you have never seen before will pass before your eyes. Adventures untold. But you must not tarry, or you will become lost in the spell of the woods as well."

He stepped to the side of the road in his odd, jerky way, his robes billowing around him. The coachman cracked his whip, and the carriage rumbled forward.

"Oh, look!" Terri gasped, pointing out her window. Everyone turned to look where she pointed.

There, at some distance from them, a white gauzy figure seemed to float in midair. Then it moved quickly, skimming through the air, at least fifteen feet off the ground.

"What is that?" Bryce asked, leaning out the window to stare at it.

Angela smiled. That was one trick she'd seen before. Most of the things Tim did were new, but some of the really successful ones he often repeated. For this one, she knew, they had strung cables with a pulley from a pole across to an old tree, and the apparition, dressed in white robes and veil, sprinkled with sparkles, was attached to the top cable by a harness he wore beneath the robe. At the appropriate time, he released a catch on the harness that let it slide along the cable, which was slanted slightly downward, until he reached the other end. Once the carriage passed him, he then pulled himself back into place with the lower cable.

"I don't know," Angela said mysteriously. "It depends on the viewer. Some people think it's a ghost, and others are certain it's an angel."

"Look over there!" Stephen said in delight, looking out the window on the other side of the carriage.

"Fairies!" Angela exclaimed with glee.

In a clearing, small silvery creatures with wings on their backs danced in a ring, a strategically placed light in a nearby tree casting a glow over them. Bryce grinned, watching them, then looked eagerly ahead for the next vision.

Next they saw two knights fighting each other on foot, and after that, a leprechaun perched on a pot of gold. Then there was a lone Indian, sitting on his horse. After that, inside a ring resembling Stonehenge several women in white were chanting and swaying while a green-clad priest raised his hands to the sky. Right after that they came upon an old crone cavorting in front of a huge caldron. She flung her hands toward it, and the flames soared up around the big pot in shades of blue and green. Finally they passed a seaweed-draped rock on which sat several lovely, long-haired mermaids, holding out their arms and beckoning to them while high, eerie voices sang.

Angela knew that by day, in a car, the drive from the gates up to Tim's front door took only a brief time and that the wooded landscape was attractive and rural, but rather ordinary. However, at night, with Tim's array of tricks, it seemed like a magical world unto itself.

When they passed the rock, there was the wizard again, nodding to them from the side of the road, saying in the same strange voice, "You have passed the Woods of Enchantment. Now you are once again in the world."

All of them relaxed, leaning back against the carriage seats.

"Quite a show," Stephen said. "Although, you know, I think last year was a little more exciting. That pirate ship and all."

Just then a dark-clad rider burst out of the trees and came racing toward them. A long black cape flowed behind him, and his lower face was covered by a black scarf. A black tricornered hat sat atop his head. He fired a dueling pistol in the air and shouted, "Stand and deliver!"

Across from them Terri let out a nervous giggle.

"Goodness," Angela remarked. "A highwayman, yet. I guess the fun isn't quite over."

They all peered out the windows to see what would happen. The coach rumbled to a halt. The highwayman waved his pistol toward the coachman and yelled, "Get out, all of you, or 'twill go the worse for him."

"I wonder if he realizes that a dueling pistol only carried one shot?" Bryce mused as Stephen reached over and opened the door.

Angela cast him a disgusted look and moved over to the door to climb out. "Don't bring reality into this."

Bryce smiled and followed the others out of the carriage.

"Ah," the highwayman was saying, leering terribly at Terri and Angela. "We have some pretty ones tonight. It's always nice to get more than money, my ladies."

"Am I going to have to defend your honor?" Bryce murmured in Angela's ear.

Just then the blunderbuss thundered above them, making all of them jump. With a cry, the figure on the horse swayed back, clutching his chest. The horse turned and pounded off, the would-be thief, now slumping forward against the horse's neck.

"There ye go," the footman cried. "It's death to any man who attacks his lordship's coach. Best get back in the vehicle now, ladies, gentlemen. We won't want to be here if any of his cronies show up."

They got back into the carriage, exclaiming over the highwayman's attack, laughing and a little breathless.

"I love Tim's parties," Stephen Jenesky said as the carriage pulled up at last in front of Tim's house.

"They're great," Angela agreed.

Bryce said nothing. He was too busy staring in amazement at Tim's house. It resembled nothing so much as a small castle. Made of dark red-brown brick, it was crammed full of towers, turrets and crenellations. There was even a decorative row of cross-shaped arrow slits near the top.

"I'm surprised there isn't a moat and drawbridge," Bryce said dryly, and Angela chuckled.

"Tim wanted to, but fortunately Melanie dissuaded him."

As they got out of the carriage, a chilling moan rent the air, and they looked up to see a white-clad figure walking along the roof, wringing her hands.

"Every castle has to have a ghost," Stephen Jenesky explained.

"I don't think I've ever seen anything so elaborate," Bryce said as two doormen dressed in Turkish costume silently swung open the double front doors for them. "Not for a party."

"Tim spends a fortune on it every year. He always has to outdo himself. Are you enjoying yourself so far?"

"You know, I think I am."

A medieval page came forward and led the other couple down a hallway. As Bryce and Angela started to follow, another page stepped up and motioned to them to stop. Minutes later, he beckoned to them, and they walked down the same hall after him.

"What now?" Bryce asked, looking at Angela with raised brows.

Angela shrugged. "Who knows? He told me he had something different for the party this year."

The young boy came to a stop in front of a door. "Through this door lies the maze, my lord and lady."

"A maze?"

"Yes, my lord. 'Tis a test of skill with riddles. To find your way through it, you must answer the clues."

"Oh, great," Bryce said with a mock groan. "You mean we could wind up lost all evening?"

Angela grinned up at him. "Only if we can't figure out the clues."

He smiled back at her, his gray eyes suddenly warm. "I can think of worse things than being lost in the dark with you."

Angela felt heat stealing through her at his words. She was suddenly very aware of the fact that she was holding Bryce's hand. *When had that happened? Had he taken her hand or had it been the other way around?* She thought about pulling it away, but then it occurred to her that that would only make it more obvious. Flustered, she turned away quickly and led him through the door.

Eight

"This is the door to his garage," Angela explained as they walked through. "I saw a tent in front of his garage, so I guess the maze extends into that."

They were in a small room with soft walls, and on each side there were flaps that could be lifted and entered. Above one flap was a purple tassel and above the other a red one. A sign hung on the wall in front of them.

Bryce leaned forward to examine the words of the sign. "Mix a crane and the name of our latest hit. Then you'll know which door to choose."

"Well, our latest game is *Code Blue,*" Angela said immediately. "You mix blue with white? Aren't cranes white? White and blue would make...pale blue?" She looked up at the tassels. "No blue. Well, I guess that's out."

Bryce stared at the wall consideringly. Suddenly he grinned. "How about a Crane, capital *C*. As in Stephen Crane's *The Red Badge of Courage?*"

Angela smiled back. "As in red and blue—purple?"

"You got it."

"Okay, let's try it."

He lifted the flap, and Angela stepped through into a narrow corridor. Fog seemed to rise from the floor, and reeds stuck up here and there, as if in a swamp.

Cautiously they made their way along the hallway, expecting at any moment for the floor to give way beneath them. Instead, when they were halfway down the little corridor, a hand, dripping with moss shot up from the floor. Bryce choked back an oath. They skirted the hand, which then slid back down beneath the fog, and arrived at another flap door. Next to Angela, a low tunnel led off. They looked at the flap, then bent to peer into the low, rounded corridor.

A small square of paper on the wall advised them to follow the path of love. Bryce looked at Angela in perplexity.

"That's easy," Angela told him. "The Tunnel of Love. Let's take this one."

"All right. I'm game."

They got down on their hands and knees and began to crawl along the tunnel.

So they went on, crawling, standing, even climbing over low barricades, and in each new place there was another "clue" to guide them. Once they could not figure out the riddle and had to retrace their steps when they reached a dead end.

A half hour later they emerged from the "maze," laughing and talking and flushed with adrenaline.

They were on a black-topped area, and there was a table of refreshments in front of them. Behind the table stood two costumed servers, who quickly and efficiently poured them drinks. Several other guests who had emerged from the maze were standing around chatting and partaking of refreshments: saloon girls, Indians, Romans, even a Hester Prynne in a Puritan costume with a large red *A* fastened on her chest.

Bryce and Angela chatted and sipped at their drinks, eyeing the other entertaining costumes as they made their way around to the side entrance of the house along a marked path and entered the party.

Spread out in front of them was a large room packed with people pulsing to the sound of a rock band. Bryce noticed that the band, set up on a small stage on one side of the enormous room, was also in costume. Then Tim came bustling up to them, dressed in the brown gown of a friar.

"Angela! And you managed to get Bryce to come, too!" Tim greeted Angela with a hug. "Wow, you look stunning."

"Thank you." Angela inclined her head with a regal nod. "Are you Friar Tuck this year?"

Tim grimaced. "No, you Philistine. That must be the hundredth time somebody's said that. Don't any of you people read? See these vials of herbs on my belt? I'm Brother Cadfael—you know, the Ellis Peters mysteries."

"Oh, yeah. Of course. I should have known you'd never be anyone as ordinary as Friar Tuck." She glanced around at the crush of people. "Your usual great party, Tim."

"Thanks." Tim's eyes lit up. "How'd you like the fairies?"

"They were wonderful."

Tim beamed. "I think this is Phil's best work yet. He even improved on the flying banshee."

"Phil is a set designer for one of the local theaters," Angela explained to Bryce. "Tim always hires him to put his visions into reality."

"He's a genius." He turned toward Bryce. "So—how are you doing? Found anything yet?"

"Well, actually, I have come across a few names that received substantial payments last year, but not the year before. I'd like to have you and Angela look at the names and see if you recognize them."

A pained expression passed across Tim's face. "Oh, no, not now. It's a party. We'll look at them on Monday." He looked past them. "New arrivals. I have to go play host. You two dance. Have some food—it's quite a spread."

He bustled off with a cheery wave of his hand.

"Not too big on facing reality, is he?"

"Who wants to hear bad news?" Angela countered. "I don't, either. Come on, let's dance."

Bryce looked at the crush on the tiny dance floor, then back at Angela. He rolled his eyes, but gamely took her hand and plunged through the mob to the dance floor.

They had barely started dancing when the song ended. It was followed by a slow dance. Bryce folded Angela in his arms, and they moved to the music. It was hot pressed up against Bryce's body, but Angela didn't mind. Even through her stiff, heavy bodice, she could feel Bryce's hard chest pressing against her. Her breasts tightened in response. One of his hands held hers, and the other was splayed across her back. Angela wondered if it was the heat or his nearness that was making her feel a trifle faint.

When the music ended, she stepped back abruptly, aware that her face was flushed. She hoped he would attribute it to the heat, not the arousal that was creeping through her.

"Why don't we go outside?" she asked quickly. "It's horribly hot in here. This brocade is beautiful, but it's stifling."

Bryce nodded, and they wound through the other revelers to the open French doors.

Apparently several other people had found the outdoor air appealing, for the flagstone terrace, decorated with soft globes of light, held several other couples.

They got glasses of punch at the refreshment table and sampled a few of the delicious dishes. Then Angela led Bryce across the patio to the terraced flagstone walk that dropped gradually down to the yard below them. Short lights lined the pathway into the yard, and party lights glittered festively in the trees.

They strolled around the pool, mutedly glowing with underwater lights, and onto the twisting graveled pathways at the rear at the yard.

"It's beautiful out here," Bryce commented, glancing around.

It was darker, the yard less manicured and the vegetation growing more naturally. Lights glowed here and there, spotlighting the trunks of occasional trees, but the winding gravel paths were unlit.

"Yes. Isn't it? Tim owns several acres." She gestured in front of them. "He's left most of the land out there as is. He and his kids like to go hiking and exploring in it. I like this part—the transition between the formal lawns and the wilderness.''

They reached a rise, where a low stone bench sat beneath a tree, and Angela turned and looked back toward the house. They were above the pool and the lower stretch of green lawn, with the brightly lit terrace and house at some distance across from them. It was almost like watching actors upon a stage to see the partygoers milling around on the terrace, with the two of them cozily alone in the dark. The sound of laughter and the band floated across the lawn toward them.

Bryce turned and looked down at her. The moonlight drifted over her, catching the row of seed pearls that lined her snood and fell across the white expanse of her chest. Her skin was soft and milky, the swell of her breasts inviting. His fingers itched to reach out and slide across her chest, to delve down into the dress. He found himself wondering what her nipples would look like—large warm brown circles or tight little raspberry buds.

Bryce swallowed and looked away. Such thoughts were dangerous, especially out here alone with Angela in the moonlight. This was her world, not his, a place of fantasy and enchantment, where people dressed like someone out of a story and the night was soft and warm and smelled faintly of romantic scents.

"I'm not sure why I came here tonight," he admitted, studying the path beneath his feet.

"That's all right. You don't always have to know exactly what you're doing. Instincts take over sometimes."

"I've never trusted instincts. They too often lead one astray."

"Perhaps we ought to go back inside," Angela suggested.

"No. I like it right here." Bryce raised his head and looked at her. "Do you?"

Angela gazed back at him. Her eyes were dark in the dim light, pools of mystery and delight. Slowly she reached up and laid her hand against his cheek. His skin flamed hot beneath her touch, and his eyes were bright silver.

"I don't know why," she began softly, "but I like to look at you."

"Neither do I," he responded. She could feel the movement in his cheek against her hand as he smiled a little. "It can't be half as pleasurable as looking at you."

She stroked her thumb across Bryce's cheek. His flesh was deliciously firm and warm to her touch; his skin sent tingles through her hand and straight into her body, where they pooled in dark ripples in her abdomen.

"You're not at all my type." Angela went on as her thumb traced the line of his upper lip.

He stiffened slightly at the touch, and his skin was like fire. Angela slid her thumb slowly along the curve of his lower lip. His mouth opened slightly and he took her thumb gently between his lips. He kissed her thumb, then trailed his tongue along it. Angela sucked in her breath and her hand fell abruptly away.

"No," Bryce agreed. "Nor are you mine."

His hand sank into her hair at her nape, holding her head immobilized, and he leaned toward her until his face was only inches from hers.

"I've been thinking about you all week. Wondering why I was stupid enough to walk away from you

Monday. Then telling myself I'd have to be crazy to get involved with you, that we're too different. Thinking that I'd rather be crazy than keep on wanting you . . . and not having you.''

Angela felt as if she were melting inside. His words were as sensual, as hungry, as any kiss. Her loins felt liquid and full and aching. Her feelings must have shown on her face, for Bryce let out a low groan.

''I'm tired of being sensible,'' he growled. ''To-night I don't want to be practical or rational. I don't want to be careful.'' He bent and took her lips in a hungry kiss.

Bryce could not remember ever wanting any woman with this kind of hungry intensity. His nature seemed to change when he was around her. A hundred times this past week he had told himself how right he had been to pull away from her the other day in her office; a relationship with someone as unpredictable, disorganized and flamboyant as Angela would quickly drive him insane. Yet, no matter how much he told himself he had been right, it had not eased the pain of wanting her. It had not gotten her out of his mind.

''I want to take you to bed,'' he said huskily, trailing his lips across her face to her ear. ''To feel your body under mine. Your legs around me.''

Angela was mesmerized by the heavy sensuality of his words. She could not think, could scarcely breathe, stunned by the throb of desire within her.

''You don't have to be the same to match,'' he said roughly. ''And I think we'll match just fine.''

Bryce's lips came back to hers, his tongue delving into the honeyed warmth of her mouth. His tongue stroked along hers like fire, delving and retreating. She could hear his harsh, ragged breath, and the sound stirred her. A hot, sweet ache began to blossom between her legs.

Bryce's arms were tight around her, pressing her into him until she thought she would not be able to breathe, but the embrace was not enough for him. He wanted to feel her up and down him; he wanted to touch her all over; he wanted to continue kissing her until time stopped and at the same moment he wanted to taste her body in a hundred different spots. Desire coiled and tightened within him.

Bryce lifted Angela in his arms and sat down on the bench, settling her on his lap. Her eyes widened a little with surprise at his sudden movement, but then she curled her arms around his neck and returned her kiss-softened lips to his. Her headgear was in the way, and he impatiently shoved it aside. It fell to the ground, loosening her hair, and the soft red curls tumbled to her shoulders. Bryce groaned and sank his hand into her hair, crushing the springing curls between his fingers.

His mouth consumed her and his arm curled around her back, holding her upright, as his other hand slid up the stiff cloth of her dress until his fingers reached the plush softness of the exposed tops of her breasts. A shudder of desire ran through him as his hand slipped gently over her breasts, following the curve and dip of each lush mound. Angela squeezed her legs tightly together, trying to ease the sudden pulsing eagerness there, and her lips fervently matched his hungry pressure.

Bryce's hand splayed over the expanse of her chest, then curved back down onto the quivering swell of her breast. Farther and deeper his fingers slipped, delving beneath the stiffened bodice until his fingertips found the tight bud that they sought. He moaned, and his mouth left hers to move hungrily over her face. He seized her earlobe gently between his teeth and worried it while his fingertips rolled and stroked and gently squeezed her taut nipple.

Angela whimpered, and her head lolled back, exposing her throat to his mouth. His lips trailed down her neck, kissing and nibbling the tender flesh. Then his mouth was upon her breast, sinking hungrily into her. She could feel the hard, throbbing length of his desire beneath her, and she moved against him, evoking a groan from him. He shoved down her bodice, exposing her breasts completely. He cupped one orb and gazed at it, gently rubbing his thumb across the pink-fleshed nipple.

Angela trembled all over as his warm mouth enclosed her nipple. It seemed as if every nerve in her body was alive and throbbing. Nothing had ever felt as wondrous, as right, as his mouth on her breast. His tongue rubbed slowly, sensuously over her nipple, and the taut bud prickled. Dampness pooled between her legs, and she wanted suddenly, wantonly, to feel his hand there.

She clenched her hands in Bryce's hair, moaning his name. His response was to suckle more deeply, sending a shudder of desire through her. His hand sought out her other breast, pushing down the cloth that covered it, and he squeezed it gently, rolling the nipple between his forefinger and thumb.

"Sweet mercy," he said in a choked voice, raising his head and gazing into her eyes. "I want to take you right here."

Angela shivered. His hand was still unconsciously caressing her breast, evoking tremors of desire in her. "What if I said yes?"

His nostrils widened fractionally, and something wild and hungry flared in his eyes. In answer, his hand went to the zipper in the back of her costume and began to pull it down. Angela stared into his eyes in fascination; this was an entirely different man from the one she had always known. This was no creature of reason, no cautious, practical, sober man. No, this was a man of passion now, impatient and unthinking, drunk on the wine of his own desire.

"Bryce," she whispered, a wealth of yearning in her voice.

Her loosened gown slid down off her shoulders, but Angela caught it, holding it up with one hand, a final remnant of sanity stopping her. "No, wait. Not here."

She glanced back toward the house, and Bryce followed her gaze. He groaned, but nodded. She was right. There were too many people not far away, too great a chance of discovery. Besides, the hard ground was hardly a fit place to make love with Angela for the first time.

"Then where?" he rasped, thinking with dismay of the long drive back to her condominium.

Angela stood up, her mind racing through the possibilities. She turned her back to him to rezip her dress. Instead he slipped his hands beneath the cloth, caressing her, and began to kiss his way up the line of her backbone.

She jumped at the first searing touch of his lips, uttering a startled little, "Oh!"

He murmured a soothing response against her skin, his hands busily at work.

"Bryce! Stop it! I'm trying to think!"

"I'm not stopping you." His tongue trailed up several vertebrae.

Angela made a choked noise. Her mind whirled. She thought that no one was likely to come up here for the next few minutes.

One of his hands slipped down, delving beneath her petticoats, and found the moist center of her desire. Bryce groaned, and his teeth nipped lightly at her back.

"I can't wait," he rasped. "I have to have you now."

He pulled his hands away, and Angela protested weakly, shocked at the loss. But then his hands went beneath her skirts, sliding caressingly up her legs and over her hips. He grasped her panties and pulled them down and off. With his hands on her hips, he turned her around to face him, and Angela moved docilely, too flooded with desire and excitement to do anything else. Bryce's face was slack with desire, his silvery eyes glittering in the moonlight. The fierce hunger on his face completed her undoing. Angela moved her hand away from her dress, letting the bodice fall. Her nipples puckered even more as the night breeze touched them. Bryce's eyes moved avidly over her, then he pulled her closer. His tongue circled each nipple teasingly, until they were engorged and throbbing and Angela's breath was almost a sob. Then he took one nipple fully into his mouth, sucking deeply.

A deep throb of desire surged through her abdomen, and Angela moved her legs restlessly. As if in answer to her unspoken wish, Bryce slid his hands up beneath her heavy skirt. He caressed her legs and buttocks, and all the while his mouth worked wonders upon her breasts. Angela was reeling with sensations, the pulse between her legs growing more and more insistent. Then his hand was there, sliding up the inside of her thigh until it came to rest upon the heated center of her being.

She moaned and twined her hands through Bryce's hair, clenching them as the heat swelled within her. Gently his fingers explored the slick, satiny folds, stroking her with fire until she was almost wild.

Then his hands were gone, and she gasped, frustrated and aching. "No! Please..."

She looked down at him. His face was flushed with passion, his eyes bright and wild. "Sit," he told her hoarsely, putting his hands on her hips and pulling her down upon him.

For a dazed instant, Angela gazed at him blankly, but then understanding dawned upon her. Lifting her skirts, she knelt on the bench, her legs on either side of his and sank slowly down onto his lap. His manhood was thick and firm, prodding deliciously at her soft femininity. His hand moved beneath her skirts and then he was sliding into her. Angela arched her head back and gripped Bryce's shoulders with her hands, easing down slowly, enjoying every frisson of pleasure as he filled her, until finally she was seated flush against him.

He groaned out her name, and his hands moved restlessly over her back. Experimentally Angela wriggled, and he gasped, burying his face in her shoulder. His fingers dug into her hips, urging her to movement. Slowly she began to move up and down, encouraged by the fevered words that fell from his lips. Her hips began to churn faster and faster, driven by the growing urgency within her. A fire coiled and tightened within her, and suddenly it burst gloriously into flames, consuming her. Bryce cried out hoarsely, muffling his cry against her skin, and she felt him buck beneath her, and for a single moment they were lost together in a white-hot explosion of desire.

Angela clung to Bryce in the aftermath of her explosive pleasure, her head nestled on his shoulder. She smiled to herself, remembering her words to Kelly only the week before. No, Bryce definitely did not have sex wearing starched, ironed pajamas.

Nine

––––

"Are you sure there's anything up here?" came the high-pitched, peevish voice of a woman, startling Angela and Bryce from their blissful inertia.

As a man's low voice mumbled something in reply, Angela's head snapped up from where she had been resting, exhausted and sated, upon Bryce's shoulder, and she looked down into his face, her mouth an *O* of horror. He stared back at her with the same expression of astonishment and dismay. Then their moment of mutual paralysis broke, and Angela scrambled off his lap. They took to their heels, awkwardly trying to straighten their clothes as they ran, and ducked behind a thicket of shrubs a short distance from where they had been.

"Did you hear something?" asked the same plaintive voice. Angela and Bryce peered through the shrubs and saw a harem girl step cautiously into the clearing they had just vacated.

"Don't be silly, Heather. Nobody's up here."

Angela covered her mouth to stifle her giggles. She glanced over at Bryce. His eyes brimmed with the same amusement. He looked utterly relaxed, satisfied, and incredibly handsome. Angela kissed him quickly.

"There! I'm sure I heard something. This place is spooky."

"Oh, for Heaven's sake, it's lovely. All right, all right, we'll go back down to the party."

In another moment the couple was gone, and Angela let out a gusty sigh of relief and sank to the ground, still holding her dress up against her bare chest. Bryce sat down beside her, his eyes twinkling.

"The things you get me into," he scolded teasingly.

"*I* get *you* into?" Angela retorted with mock indignation.

"Absolutely. I would never have done anything this reckless if you weren't so damn desirable." He leaned over and kissed her.

"Well," Angela said, smiling, "if you put it like that..."

He pulled her into his arms and they lay back on the ground, gazing up at the clear night sky.

"Isn't it perfect?" Angela sighed.

"Mmm." Bryce's voice was laced with amusement. "A bench for a bed. Almost being discovered *en flagrante*. Twigs in your hair." He reached up and took a tiny twig from the bush that had become entangled in Angela's wildly tumbling hair.

"Like I said, absolutely perfect."

"Where's your hat, by the by?" Bryce asked, idly playing with a lock of her tangled hair.

Angela clapped her hands to her head. "Oh, my gosh, it's back there somewhere. It's a wonder that couple didn't see it." She began to giggle.

"I think she was too eager to get away to see anything. No doubt she suspected he had some nefarious motive in bringing her up here."

"Mmm. Like you?"

"Like me," he agreed equably. "What?" he said at her startled glance. "You think I didn't know what I was doing? I told you, I've thought about you all week, and I realized there was nothing for me to do but surrender."

"Surrender? As if I'd been trying to catch you!"

"I was hoping you would. Finally it became obvious that I'd have to come to you. You used to be more persistent, you know, when you were younger."

Angela made a face at him, and he chuckled. "Come on." He sat up, lifting her with him. "Turn around and I'll zip you up."

He followed his words with action, adding a kiss on her nape when he had finished.

"Thank you." Angela felt suddenly, strangely, shy with him, as if, encased once again in her costume, she was now a stranger.

"My pleasure."

Angela smiled at him with a trace of awkwardness. "I must look a mess."

"You look beautiful," he assured her softly as his hand stroked her hair. Sensing her mood, he pulled her into his arms and cuddled her, his cheek resting against her hair. Angela relaxed with a sigh and snuggled into his chest, her arms going around his waist.

"Is there any way we can sneak out of here?" he asked finally. "I want to be alone with you."

Angela pulled away and smiled at him. Her face was radiant, and she looked to him even more breathtakingly lovely. "Of course. I'm a master at sneaking out."

Bryce retrieved her snood from where it lay in front of the bench, slightly trampled, and Angela took him by the hand and led him through the trees to another path that went down the hill, skirting Tim's house. The trail wound its way through trees, bushes, and clearings, sometimes almost indiscernible even in the full moonlight. Bryce strolled amiably along, holding Angela's hand, less concerned with the prospect of getting lost than with the strange, wonderful feeling that had taken hold of him. He felt marvelously relaxed and content—almost giddy, in fact, and it seemed to him at that moment not at all unusual to be creeping away from a party along a dirt track through the trees, dressed in full costume, having just made love in a secluded copse of trees.

He doubted that he had ever done anything quite as impulsive, but it seemed only right, somehow, with Angela. Not that the idea of making love to her in a traditional way didn't have its appeal; it was a prospect he was contemplating with considerable interest at the moment. He glanced over at Angela. The moonlight silvered her fair skin and darkened the fire of her tumbled hair. Her lips were full and soft, with the faintly bruised look of a mouth that had been kissed recently and thoroughly. Just looking at her mouth brought the heat of desire darting through his loins again. He thought of her hair spread out across his pillow, a tangle of blazing curls, of her body, white and naked beneath his. Yes, the idea of having the time and the leisure to explore every aspect of making love to Angela was sounding more attractive every second.

Bryce pulled her to a stop, and Angela glanced at him inquiringly. He pulled her close and kissed her, tasting the sweetness of her lips as if he'd never known it before. Angela pressed eagerly into him.

Finally he lifted his face, though his body was still as close as a heartbeat to hers. "Are you sure we're going the right way?" he asked a little breathlessly, brushing a lock of hair from her face with caressing fingers.

"Yes." Angela smiled. "I'm positive. Don't trust me, huh?"

"It's not that. It's just that . . . I'd like very much to get back to your apartment."

Angela's smile deepened sensually. "Don't worry. We will. I'd like to get back there, too."

They started off again, plunging into a mass of dark trees, but, amazingly, when they came through the thicket, there on the other side were rows of parked cars. They were at the bottom of Tim's lot, where they had parked. Within minutes, they were in Bryce's car and on their way back to Angela's condominium. They held hands as he drove, and Angela noticed that Bryce's driving was even swifter this time than it had been coming over.

When they reached her complex, they almost ran up the stairs and arrived breathless and panting at her doorstep. With fingers that shook, Angela fitted her key into the door, hoping that this would not be one of those nights when Jim stuck his head out of the next door, calling her in for a cup of chamomile tea and a chat.

The condo next door remained blessedly dark and quiet, and in a moment, Angela had the door open and they were inside.

They made their way through her home to the bedroom in back, pausing to kiss and caress or to slip a garment off. They left a trail behind them of discarded shoes, jacket, dress and petticoats as they went from living room to Angela's bedroom. They paused to kiss and cling to each other, only to break away to take off another garment, then returned to the embrace, so that it took a long time to reach their destination. But finally they tumbled onto the bed, naked and entwined.

Somewhat sated by their earlier lovemaking, they did not rush to completion this time, but made love slowly, lingeringly, giving their time to the sweet enjoyment of every movement, every expression, every inch of their lover's flesh. They kissed and caressed, murmuring endearments and soft words of delight, until the passion rose in them so fiercely that they could not hold back. Caught up in the hungry rush of desire, they moved together, clinging frantically, until at last pleasure exploded within them, even sweeter and more intense than it had been the first time.

They relaxed, still holding each other, and Bryce reached back and grabbed a handful of the comforter, which lay atop Angela's bed and pulled it around them to ward off the chill of the air against their damp bodies. Cocooned in its warmth, nestled snugly together, they drifted into sleep.

* * *

The familiar strains of the Concordia theme awakened Angela. She opened her eyes, blinking sleepily, disoriented for a moment. It struck her that someone was in her house, and for a moment she tensed with fear. Then she remembered that Bryce was here.

He must be playing the Concordia game. It seemed unlikely...but then everything that had happened with Bryce had been a surprise. A slow smile curved Angela's lips as she remembered the night before. Perhaps Bryce was not the man for her, as she had been telling herself in vain for the past week, but they had made love as if they were perfectly matched. No other man had ever touched her as deeply or as quickly.

Angela sat up, shoving her thick hair back from her face, and pulled her knees up to her chin, wrapping her arms around her jackknifed legs, as if she could hug her happiness to her. *Could she actually be falling in love with Bryce?* A few weeks ago she would have laughed at the idea, but it seemed quite possible now. Even a week ago she had been telling herself all the reasons why it would never work, why she should not give in to her yearnings. But this morning she could not think of a one. She felt happier and lighter, freer, than she had anytime since the IRS had descended upon H & A Enterprises.

After a few moments of blissful reverie, she got up and went into the bathroom to shower. She came back into the bedroom, a terry-cloth robe tied around her and a turbaned towel wrapped around her wet hair. She padded out the door and across the landing to the second bedroom, which served as her office.

The room was crammed full of bookcases, all stuffed with books and game boxes and assorted odds and ends that she had collected through the years, such as a lopsided pot made for her by one of her nephews in third-grade art class, a breathtaking metal sculpture of an eagle swooping down to seize its prey, and a jumbled collection of calling cards that she had picked up at various trade shows and never taken the time to sort out. Her desk, with its computer equipment, took up most of the wall beneath the window, and it was here that Bryce sat, frowning at the screen.

Angela slipped up behind him and crossed her arms over his chest, bending down to kiss the top of his head. She could feel his body relax beneath her, and he tilted back his head to smile up at her.

"Did I wake you? I'm sorry. I hadn't realized that this thing had music until I turned it on." He stretched up and kissed her lightly on the lips.

"It has everything," Angela replied and kissed him again, more lingeringly. "Anyway, I didn't mind waking up."

Bryce slid the chair back from the desk and pulled Angela around the chair and into his lap. "How are you feeling this morning?" he asked, his eyes searching hers. "Do you regret last night?"

"Of course not," Angela replied indignantly, then added more hesitantly, "Do you?"

"No. I enjoyed every minute of it thoroughly."

"Good." Angela smiled and snuggled down against his shoulder. "Me, too. I feel too good to analyze it."

He released her hair from the towel, brushing the wet strands from her face with his hand. They sat for a moment in silence. Angela thought lazily that it felt wonderful to sit like this with Bryce, cozy and comfortable, yet still charged with an undercurrent of excitement. She knew that if she made any movement

toward him, reached out to caress his arm or to kiss
the deep hollow at the base of his throat—both of
which tempted her—that they would be back in her
bed shortly, making love again. The thought ap-
pealed to her, but for the moment, she was content
simply to be close to him. There would be plenty of
time for lovemaking later.

"What got into you, to come in here and start
playing a game?" she asked.

She could feel his shrug beneath her cheek. "I'm
not sure," he said. "I was awake and I thought I'd do
some work to pass the time while you slept. I came in
here, but all I could find were these games. So I decided to try one, see what they were like. After all, I
seem to have taken on a new, impulsive persona
lately." He paused, then said in a softer voice, "I
thought I might get some insight into you if I played
one."

There was a silence, and finally Angela said,
"Well?"

"Well, what? Oh, did I find out anything about
you? Not much. Except that I realized that the game
was just as frustrating as you are."

"Well! That's a nice thing to say!" Angela exclaimed with mock indignation, sitting up and twisting to face him, but her eyes were dancing and her
voice was rich with laughter.

"Sorry," he replied with equally amused insincer-
ity, leaning over to kiss her on the tip of her nose. "I
meant to say, intriguing."

"That's better."

"How the hell do you play the damn thing?" he
asked, some of his recent exasperation creeping into
his voice.

Angela stood up and perched on the narrow arm of the chair, gazing at the screen. "Oh, you're playing IV, right? The Silver Mountains one?"

"Yes. And all I do is walk, but everywhere I go, some big bird swoops down and eats me or I fall in a swamp or I go by a talking rock and on and on into a forest. There are two trails in it, but I get killed both ways. And if I don't go into the woods, I wind up going around this college and winding up at the same place as one of the other trails, where I get killed again."

Angela had to chuckle at his outraged expression. "Did you look at the hints manual?"

"Hints manual? You mean you need a book in order to play this thing?"

"Not necessarily, but it makes it easier. Although we try to make our aid books vague enough that you still have to figure it out."

"And people do this for enjoyment?"

Angela had to laugh at his skeptical expression. "It's fun, I promise. You just have to figure out the kind of things you have to do, and once you realize how to think, it gets positively addictive."

"If you say so."

"I say so. See, the thing is that this guy, Sir Leopold, has to rescue the good sorceress, Ermina, from the wicked King Grilvag, who lives at the top of the highest peak of the Silver Mountains. But it's a long way there, and the only way he can make it is to pick up things along the way and put them in his knapsack. Later, when he needs to, he can use them or give them to someone in exchange for something."

"What things?"

"Well, for instance, at the talking rock, Leopold can pick up a golden hammer. If you pay attention to the riddle the rock says, it tells you where to go. You go there, and there's the hammer."

Angela stood up and bent over the desk, using the mouse to maneuver the figure on the screen along a path. The rock spoke, and she glanced back expectantly at Bryce. His eyes had drifted to her derriere, which, in the position she was standing, was outlined prominently beneath her robe.

"Uh, Bryce..." Angela snapped her fingers.

Bryce turned his gaze back to her face, smiling sheepishly. "What? Oh." He looked at the scene for a moment, then said, "I'm sorry. I'm afraid I got, uh, distracted. What did you say?"

Angela couldn't keep from smiling as she touched the rock again and it repeated its words.

Bryce gazed at her blankly and started to shake his head. Then his eyes lit up. "Oh, wait, I see. Round age—the rings of a tree, right? And pages in a book— leaves. It's talking about a big tree. And 'grandfather of them all'—it must be the big one over there."

"Exactly. So now we move Sir Leopold over to the tree." She leaned over again, demonstrating with the mouse.

The figure walked in its stiff way across the screen to the tree, and a lively little piece of music came on. Sir Leopold looked up. A golden hammer glittered in the branches. Bryce glanced at it, but then his gaze was drawn inexorably back to Angela's backside, so tantalizingly close.

"Now you have to click on this button up here," Angela went on. "That makes him touch what's in front of him."

Angela clicked, and the knight moved jerkily to recover the hammer and look at it.

Bryce stretched his hand down and put it on her leg, slowly sliding it up under her robe.

Angela jumped, giggling. "Bryce!" She turned to look at him with feigned outrage, but she could not hide the sensual warmth that lit her eyes at his touch. "Now pay attention."

He grinned. "Yes, ma'am." But his hand did not stop its upward journey until his fingers curved over her bare buttock. His eyes darkened sensually as he realized that Angela was naked beneath her robe.

"You're not paying attention," Angela said a trifle breathlessly as his hand caressed her bottom.

"I am," Bryce protested. "I'm paying very close attention."

"To the screen, I mean."

"Oh. That. All right." He turned his head to look at the monitor, but his hand did not stop its smooth caress. "Go ahead."

Angela turned back to the screen and went on. "You have to put the hammer into his knapsack. You, uh, push the icon that looks like a . . ." She sucked in her breath as his fingers slid over the curve of her derriere and between her legs.

"Like a what?" Bryce asked in a low voice as his fingers gently probed the gates of her femininity.

"A bag. A drawstring bag." Angela got out the words. She could feel the moisture pooling between her legs, inviting his further caresses.

"Okay. Now what?"

"Bryce . . ." she protested faintly, but she widened er stance, allowing his magical fingers easier access.

"Mmm-hmm?" He found and stroked the small nub of flesh that sent tendrils of electric pleasure through her. "Go ahead."

Angela looked distractedly at the screen, trying to remember what she was doing. There was something very titillating about continuing with her demonstration while Bryce's hand caressed her. "Well, you keep the hammer in your bag until you find something that looks like you could use the hammer—or trade it." She drew in her breath sharply as his other hand shoved the back of her robe up and Bryce bent to kiss her hip. "Uh, I mean, you know, to get something you want."

Bryce nipped gently at the soft flesh of her buttock, murmuring, "Like what?"

"Huh? Oh. Well, say, if you reach the Silver Mountains and run into a gnome, he'd like to have the hammer to use in mining the silver vein."

"Why?" His voice was husky, his breath hot against her naked flesh.

"Why?" Angela repeated blankly. Bryce's finger was stroking her rhythmically, slowly, making her feel swollen and achy. "Well, uh, that's what the gnomes do. Mine. And he will let you pass if you offer him the—" She let out a groan as the heat knotted within her "—the—ah—"

She broke off, letting go of the computer mouse and grasping the monitor with both hands. "Oh, Bryce..."

"I get it," he said hoarsely, gently increasing the pressure of his finger.

"But first," Angela managed to gasp out. "Remember to save it."

"Right. Save first," he murmured as his mouth moved up her back. He reached around and jerked loose the sash tying her robe. It fell open, and he cupped her breast.

Angela made an inarticulate noise as his hands and mouth worked on her, bombarding her with pleasure. She murmured his name, gripping the monitor tightly, as desire coiled and tightened in her abdomen, pushing her ever closer to the brink.

She cried out as he pushed her over that edge, tumbling her into a void of hot, black passion. For a moment there was nothing but him and the heat that seared through her, releasing and enslaving her all at the same time.

Slowly Angela drifted down from the heights of passion. She turned to Bryce, her face slack and glowing with sated desire.

"Oh, Bryce," she whispered. "That was..." She groped for words adequate to describe the pleasure that had flooded her being.

"Wait," he said with a wicked grin, reaching out and pulling her toward him. "It's not over yet."

Ten

─────

"I guess that's true." Angela smiled sensually as she reached out and took Bryce's hands, pulling him to his feet. "Now I get to return the favor, right?"

Languid and sated, she looked forward to spending a long time arousing and satisfying Bryce. Angela could see that Bryce was already well aroused. That wasn't nearly enough, though, for her. She wanted him to be as captured, as much on fire, as she had been.

She began to unbutton his shirt, trailing her fingernails down the skin as it was revealed. "You don't look like someone who sits behind a desk all day playing with numbers."

"I work out."

"Mmm. No doubt that's the practical thing to do."

He smiled faintly. "No doubt."

"It also looks very attractive." Angela had finished undoing his shirt and she pushed it back and off his shoulders, revealing his wide chest.

"Why, thank you, ma'am." He opened his eyes and looked at her. His eyes sparkled with humor, but behind that lay a hotter flame.

Angela slid her hands over his shoulders and across the hard thrust of his collarbone, then moved down his chest, following the line of dark hair to where it disappeared in the waistband of his trousers. She ran a fingertip along the edge of the waistband and moved back up his chest, caressing his ribs and teasing the flat nipples to life, tangling her fingertips among the curling hairs.

Bryce stifled a groan of pleasure as she explored his body, and Angela felt his manhood swell and press beneath her. His cheeks were flushed with desire. Stretching up, she kissed him, her tongue delving into his mouth, and as her lips played against his, her fingers roamed his arms and chest. Bryce slid his hands up her thighs, digging his fingers into her hips when a new onslaught of pleasure hit him. When at last their lips parted, Angela slid down his body to trace with her tongue the path her fingers had traveled over and around his masculine nipples.

Bryce tightened, making an inarticulate noise, and Angela looked up. "I'm sorry. Did I—"

"No," he gasped. "Don't stop. Don't ever stop."

"But I have to," Angela said. "or how would I be able to do this?"

Her lips left his nipple and traveled down the center line of his chest, gently tasting and teasing his skin. "Or this?" she added, pulling back and beginning to unfasten his trousers.

Bryce groaned and quickly moved to help her, sliding out of the rest of his clothes. They sank to the floor, and Bryce moved between her legs, slowly sliding into her. Restlessly Angela stroked his body with her hands as he began to move within her, thrusting in and pulling out again in long, teasing strokes.

Gradually his rhythm grew faster, and Angela writhed, sinking her hands into his buttocks and urging him on to completion. Then at last the pleasure burst within them, wild and glorious, so fierce that they cried aloud with it.

Bryce collapsed upon Angela, panting, and for a long moment they simply lay there, stunned by the power of their lovemaking.

Finally, in a dry voice, Bryce said, "Well. I understand now why the Concordia games are so popular."

Angela chuckled, and somehow in that moment she was certain that she had fallen in love with Bryce.

Later that day Angela took Bryce out to her house on Lake Gaston. They had gone back to his hotel so that he could change into more casual clothes than the riverboat gambler costume he had worn the night before, and he was dressed in jeans and a crisp white dress shirt with the sleeves rolled up on his forearms. Though Angela had to smile at what Bryce termed casual, she thought he also looked unbearably handsome.

The sternness in his face had softened, and when he smiled at her, there was a warmth in his gray eyes that changed him. Angela wondered why she had ever thought him stiff and pompous. *Why hadn't she realized that the cool remoteness was nothing but a façade, a front beneath which was a man capable of laughing and talking and having fun, a man who made love with fierce emotion?* But she wondered, too, if it were possible to completely crack that shell around him, to make him forget probabilities and logic and plans and give himself up to loving her. If he did not, she knew, she was laying herself open to heartbreak.

It was a beautiful day to drive through the North Carolina countryside. Fragile-looking dogwood trees and bright red buds were in full bloom, and purple wisteria vines cascaded from a tall tree or twined around a fence. Their usual wet March had brought its typical reward.

About an hour later, as they neared the Virginia border, Angela turned off the highway. A few minutes later, she took a narrow gravel road. She pulled to a stop in front of a modern stone and wood house.

"Is this your place?" Bryce asked, looking around with interest.

"Yes." Angela smiled. "But you haven't seen the best yet."

She led him inside the house and down the steps to the large common room. Almost the entire back wall consisted of glass, framing a breathtaking view of the lake. Outside, a stone patio provided an even closer look.

"It's beautiful." Bryce stepped out onto the patio, and Angela followed, sitting down on the low stone wall at the edge of the flagstones.

He sat down beside her, and she glanced up at him. "I always feel so much better when I come here. Peaceful and content, no matter how crazy the week's been at work."

"This is really your home, isn't it?" he asked as-
y.

Angela shrugged. "Yeah, I guess so. I like my condo, but it's more for convenience than anything else. I come out here every chance I get, at least a couple of weekends a month."

"I can understand why." Bryce looked around.

"Then you like it? Really?"

"Oh, yes. You're right, it's very peaceful. Soothing. I'm surprised you don't live out here full-time."

"You're the first person who's ever said that," Angela said, a little surprised. "I've thought about it many times. I could do my work here, maybe go into the office one day a week."

"Why haven't you?"

"I think because I'd miss the people. I love the solitude here, and it's great for working. But I'd get lonely. I like people, too. I'm used to talking to Kelly and Tim and all the others. I'd miss that. This way I have it both ways."

Later, after a cold lunch on the patio, they took Angela's boat out on the lake. They cruised around the lake for a while then returned and spent the rest of the afternoon on lounge chairs, watching the sun sink behind the lake and talking desultorily.

Angela, after telling a funny story about her sister and herself when they were young, looked over at Bryce and said, "You never say anything about your family. Here you know everything about me and my family, and I know hardly anything about you. Where did you grow up? What's your family like?"

She knew that she was getting into delicate territory, given what her mother had told her about Bryce's childhood, but she wanted to know more about him, to understand him.

Bryce shrugged and leaned back in his chair, closing his eyes in the sun's glare. "Nothing much to tell," he said noncommittally. "I grew up in Charlotte."

After a long pause, Angela prompted, "And . . . ?"

"And what?"

"Your family," Angela said in exasperation. "Do you have any siblings? What about your parents?"

"I have a brother and a sister. I'm the oldest." He paused for a moment, and Angela thought he was not going to say anything else, but then he went on. "My dad left us. And my mother was a drunk."

Angela went still. She could sense the ache in his carefully controlled voice, the pain that his closed eyes hid. "Oh. I'm sorry. I shouldn't pry. My big mouth, you know—it's always getting me into trouble."

"It's all right," Bryce said, opening his eyes and sitting up. "It's not your fault."

He paused for a moment, looking out over the darkening lake, then said, "Life in our house was chaotic. Half the time I'd come home from school and find my mother passed out on the couch. No supper, the younger kids running around wild. It's a wonder they never got hurt. She'd drink up my lunch money . . . or the grocery money. My father took off when I was eight. I guess he couldn't take it anymore. But I was always furious at him because he didn't take us with him."

"Oh, Bryce." Angela reached out and took his hand, squeezing it. "I'm sorry. How awful for you."

The stiffness in Bryce's body eased somewhat at her touch. "I suppose that's why I was always so interested in order and precision." He went on. "Numbers are wonderfully reliable. If you add this number _ _ _hat number, it will always come out the same answer. Things can be added and subtracted and divided, and you can be sure about it.''

"You wanted to make order out of the chaos.''

"Exactly. I kept trying to do it at home—keep Gail and Jimmy fed and going to school on time, our clothes ironed.''

"But you were just a child yourself! How could you be expected to do that?''

"I pretty much had to, or else the social worker would have taken us away from her, split us up. And however bad it was, that would have been worse. At least Mom loved us, in her own fashion . . . at least we were together.''

"So you were never really a kid.''

"I suppose not. You must think that that explains a lot about me.'' He gave her a faint smile.

"I guess it does.'' Angela tilted her head to one side consideringly. "It also makes you even more intriguing.''

"Intriguing?'' His brows rose. "I wouldn't have picked that term.''

"That's because you're the numbers guy. *I'm* the romantic one. This is my territory.''

"If you say so. But I think your claim to being a romantic may take a severe decline after being associated with me.'' He turned to look back out over the lake. "Don't picture me as some dark, sensitive hero straight out of *Wuthering Heights*. I haven't spent my life brooding over my tragic past. I knew I wanted out of there, and I laid plans to do it. I worked and saved and went to college, all according to a timetable I'd worked out.''

"I bet you did." Angela chuckled. "But that doesn't make your past any less difficult or what you did any less admirable."

"Admirable?" He quirked an eyebrow. "*You* think what I've done is admirable? I never thought I'd hear that from you."

"Well, your field isn't my kind of thing, but that doesn't mean that I wouldn't find your raising your siblings and working your way through college and becoming a success admirable. I think anyone would."

"Probably. I never felt admirable, though, I'll tell you. Most of the time I just felt driven. I knew what I wanted, and I couldn't get there fast enough."

"But you wanted more than just money."

"You think so?"

"Yes, or you wouldn't have visited my family."

He looked at her sharply. "Why not? They had everything I wanted—money, beautiful possessions, breeding, taste. All the time I was there I was soaking up knowledge."

"I don't think that was it, though—the reason why you came."

Bryce paused, then said slowly, "In part. The Hewitts seemed to me to be the perfect family. I wanted to be like them, to talk and think and act like them. To not be the raw, unpolished, *hungry* kid I was. But I also wanted . . . to be a part of that family, not just to have those things and be 'right' socially, but to belong. To have a right to that kind of love, that kind of order and reason. I guess when you accused me of trying to take your place, I really was. I didn't ~ant to displace you, but I did want very much to be of your family."

"Oh, Bryce, I was such a stinker to resent you!" Tears began to form in Angela's eyes as she thought of how lonely he must have been, how hungry and desperate for a normal family—and instead of understanding or helping him, she had been cruel to him.

Bryce smiled and pulled her into his arms. "You were just a kid. Besides, look at it this way—what could have been more like being a part of the family than having an annoying little pest of a sister?"

Angela smiled at him provocatively. "Well, actually, I'm awfully glad that I *wasn't* your little sister."

He grinned, and his hand curled around the back of her neck possessively. "So am I," he said and bent down to take her lips in a passionate kiss.

They left the lake early Monday morning. They had planned to return to Raleigh on Sunday, but they were enjoying their time at the lake so much that they kept putting off their departure and finally decided to spend Sunday night there as well.

The pale light of dawn was creeping through the sky when Angela followed Bryce out to her car. "You drive," she suggested, handing him the keys to the sports car. "I'd wreck us for sure." She succumbed to a jaw-cracking yawn, adding, "I can't imagine what I'm doing up at this hour."

Bryce just chuckled and took the keys from her. "This is the best time of the day."

He opened the small trunk of the Miata and stowed away their bags, whistling cheerfully. Angela cast him a jaundiced look and slid into the passenger side, nursing her cup of coffee.

Bryce settled into the driver's seat and proceeded to adjust it and the mirrors to precisely the right position for him. Then his eyes slid over the dashboard, locating the various switches and knobs that controlled the functions of the car. Angela watched him, smiling fondly. *How was it that Bryce's precise ways had become so endearing?* She had always suspected that love made people insane, and now she was sure of it.

She wondered if he knew that she loved him—and what he would do if he did. Somehow she could not imagine Bryce Richards falling in love in just two weeks—or admitting it if he did. They had spent the weekend intimately, both physically and verbally, talking about any- and everything. Angela had poured out her feelings and thoughts to him, letting him glimpse more of her soul than she had ever shown anyone. She was certain that he was the man she would love for the rest of her life. But she wondered if Bryce could make such a quick, deep commitment. After all, it wasn't at all logical to fall in love so quickly.

He had said nothing about love all weekend, and Angela, not wanting to scare him off, had kept her own feelings silent. She could handle that for a while. What worried Angela was that he might never feel for her what she felt for him. *What if the hard shell he had wrapped around his emotions could never be broken? What if he would never allow himself to do something as unreasonable as loving an emotional, impulsive, illogical person as herself?*

Bryce glanced over at her and smiled. Angela had barely brushed her hair this morning, and she wore no makeup. She was clad in her usual jeans and her shirt collar was turned under on one side, completing her barely together look. He thought she was utterly beautiful.

He started the car and turned up the narrow road to the highway. This weekend should have left him in turmoil, he knew. He had acted rashly, without thought for the consequences. He hadn't even remembered to leave a message at his hotel when they left for the lake, just in case someone at his business needed to reach him. For over a day he had immersed himself in passion. He had spent every moment with a woman with whom he would have sworn he had nothing in common—and yet he did not feel that it had been nearly long enough. He didn't even *feel* normal; he was almost giddy, smiling for no reason, and he was reluctant to return to work. Somehow every moment spent away from Angela seemed to be time wasted.

Everything was wrong and confused—yet he was blissfully happy.

Bryce glanced over at Angela again. He took Angela's hand in his and raised it to his lips. He decided he was not going to analyze this. Right now, he was just going to let it be.

Angela and Bryce parted reluctantly at his hotel, and she returned to her condo to shower and dress. When she arrived at work, Bryce was already deep in computer sheets in Kelly's office. He looked up when Angela stuck her head in the office, and he smiled at her in a way that turned her knees to jelly.

She thought that she would not be able to work, knowing that Bryce was just down the hall, but she was surprised to find that ideas simply flowed out of her. She was soon engrossed in her work, so much so that when someone knocked on the frame of her open door two hours later, she jumped.

She looked up and saw Bryce standing in her doorway, and a huge grin spread across her face. She was unaware that her skin glowed and her eyes sparkled, too; she was only aware of the uprush of feeling in her chest when she looked at him.

"Hi! Come in." Angela rose to her feet as he crossed the room and came around her desk.

She wanted to kiss him, and she was wondering if she ought to go close the door when Bryce reached her and bent down and kissed her. Angela quickly threw her arms around him and returned the kiss.

"I've been thinking about that all morning," Bryce said.

Angela knew she was grinning like an idiot, but she couldn't stop. "I'm glad you decided to act on it."

"Well, I did manage to make myself wait until I had an excuse to come in here."

"Oh? What?"

"I have some names I want you to look at." Bryce laid a sheet of paper down on her desk.

"Okay." Angela sat back down in her chair and studied the piece of notepaper. On it were the names of several companies, each with an address and phone number beneath it. Across from each name was a dollar amount. "What are these?"

"That's what I want you to tell me," Bryce said, perching on her desk. "Who are these companies?"

Frowning, Angela scanned the names, murmuring, "ALM, Brachen, Carswell . . . now that sounds familiar. Carswell . . . oh, I remember. That's the new name ʼr Frank Carter's company. They employ high-tech ᴽoraries, primarily for computer companies. We

had to hire some extra workers about three months last
year. We've used them before, but it was called Independent Temporary Services or something like that.
Then last year Frank joined up with another company owned by Jason Sidwell, and they named the new
one Carswell.''

"Okay." Bryce drew a line through the name.
"What about those first two? ALM or Brachen?"

Angela shook her head slowly, trying to dredge
something up from her memory. "Nope. I'm draw-
ing a blank."

"What about the others?"

Angela slowly drew her finger down the left side of
the page. "F & F Graphics—no. Nagel & Boone—I
don't know, sounds like a law firm, doesn't it? Maybe
C.P.A.'s. Tri-Cor—now that's the company that sold
us that new computer equipment last year. Are these
companies we paid money to or something?"

"Yeah. The ones that I can't find any payments to
from the year before. I'm looking for something different, see, from the other years. Something that will
account for the loss in profit. These are all fairly large
amounts. The Nagel one's the smallest."

"Doesn't ring a bell, either. It sounds sort of like a
game company or something."

Angela glanced up and saw her partner walking by
and called out, "Hey, Tim! Come here and look at
these."

"What? Hi, Angela." Tim walked obediently into
her office. "Oh, hi, Bryce. What's going on?"

"Bryce was asking me about these names. You recognize any of them?"

Tim took the list and glanced down it curiously.

"I told him what Carswell was, and I knew Tri-Cor. But the others..."

"Well, Nagel & Boone is that law firm we hired in California. You remember last year when some jerk claimed we'd stolen one of our games from him?"

"Oh, yeah, sure. The judge dismissed it." Angela looked at Bryce. "Sorry. Our attorney was actually named Silverman, that's why I didn't recognize it."

"And didn't this Woolman thing sell us the chairs in the conference room?"

Angela frowned. "I thought Marbank always supplied our office furniture."

"I don't know. Maybe you're right. But this sounds familiar."

"What about Xanadu?"

Tim shook his head. "I don't know. Why don't you ask Kelly? She's more likely to know than we are. I can ask around, see if anybody remembers."

"No," Bryce said quickly. "Don't do that. I'd just as soon we kept this to ourselves for the moment."

Tim and Angela gazed at him blankly.

"Why?" Angela asked. "I thought you wanted to find out."

Bryce grimaced. "I do. I just don't want to alert the entire company."

The confusion in Angela's and Tim's eyes changed simultaneously into astonished understanding.

"You think someone's stealing from us!"

Eleven

Bryce shrugged. "It's a possibility. If your expenses are out of line, and you all aren't making them up to avoid taxes, then someone else could be making up the expenses and pocketing the money."

"No," Tim said positively. "It's nobody here."

"Maybe not." Bryce looked unconvinced. "There may not be any theft. Every expense you've got may be legitimate, and the IRS may drop it like a hot potato. But in the meantime, I have to check out all the possibilities. And I don't want to give anybody a chance to cover their tracks. That's why I don't want any discussion of this outside this office."

"Not even with Kelly?" Tim asked.

Bryce groaned. "Not with anybody. I shouldn't even have asked *you.*"

"But surely you can't suspect Kelly," Angela protested.

Tim looked troubled. "She's been with us since the beginning, almost."

"I don't *suspect* anybody. Or anything. But I can't rule anyone or anything out yet, either. You can't expect to find the truth if you start out with a bunch of assumptions. Besides, the more people who know, the more talk there will be, and if someone is embezzling the money, we don't want to tip their hand."

Tim sighed. "All right. I won't tell Kelly. But I'm positive you're wrong."

He turned abruptly and walked off toward his office.

Bryce looked after him with a frown. "He's going to have a hard time accepting it."

"So would I," Angela responded. "I really think you're on the wrong track here. Just because I don't remember some of these names doesn't mean that someone's embezzling money from us."

"No. Not necessarily."

"How will you find out—I mean, whether these are phony companies or not?"

"Well, here's one simple way." Bryce pointed to the telephone number beneath F & F Graphics, one of the names that she and Tim had not recognized. "Call and see if it's a legitimate number."

Angela picked up the receiver and punched in the numbers. She waited, listening, and after a moment her eyes widened. She hung up the phone, looking troubled. "A recorded message came on. It said this isn't a working number."

Excitement sparked in Bryce's eyes, and he reached across the desk to take the telephone. "All right. What's the address—Greensboro?" He began to punch in numbers.

Angela fought down the panicky feeling rising in her. "Maybe they've just gone out of business."

"We'll find out. I'm calling my office. They'll check up on them."

Angela's work was ruined for the rest of the day. She could not get her mind off the possibility that someone was embezzling from them. By the middle of the afternoon, she was even too antsy to stay in the office. Every time she walked down the hall or went to the kitchen downstairs, she couldn't help looking at her employees and wondering if this one or that one were capable of stealing from them. Worse, she felt guilty for not telling Kelly about Bryce's suspicions. *Would Kelly think that she had suspected her, too?* She wished she had not told Bryce that she wouldn't confide in Kelly. Finally she gave up in disgust and drove home, stopping only to tell Bryce where she was going.

He nodded. "Okay. I haven't heard from my office yet. I'll come by your condo and let you know when I do."

It was a little bit better in her own home, but the time seemed to crawl by. She tried to read, but couldn't, and she resorted to looking at television. There was little on except talk shows, however, and after awhile, she cut the television off, too, and simply sat, staring at the wall and worrying while the afternoon turned into evening.

It was almost eight o'clock when Bryce finally rang her doorbell. Angela opened the door quickly, her stomach filled with butterflies. Bryce's face was hard and his eyes glittered. Angela knew that that was not a good sign.

"What did you find out?" she asked leadenly.

"The address for F & F is one of those mailbox stores in Greensboro. Okay, maybe they want a nicer address to impress their customers. But there's also no listing for them in the Greensboro phone book. *Last* year's phone book—when you sent them the check. So it isn't just that they've gone out of business. I also checked with the Better Business Bureau...never heard of them. Nor is there anyone registered with a dba as F & F Graphics."

"Dba?"

"Doing business as. You have to register when you do business under a name other than your own."

"Oh. Yeah. Okay. So it's definitely a phony company."

"Yeah. A $20,000 phony company."

"That's how much we paid them?"

"Yes. One of my employees in Charlotte checked out Brachen. Again, no dba registration, no listing in the phone book, no knowledge of them in the Better Business Bureau. Their address is a post office box, which anyone could rent. But this time they were a little more sophisticated. It's a voice-mail number, rented by a Mr. Deal. The voice-mail company gets paid with a money order every month, no check. They also checked San Jose for ALM, the other company that neither you nor Tim recognized. Same results."

Angela gazed at him, wide-eyed, struggling to accept his words. "So someone has stolen money from us."

"At least $200,000 over the course of the past year and a half. It's no wonder your profit margin was down."

Angela felt queasy. "It has to be one of our employees, right? I mean, someone outside the company couldn't do it?"

"I don't see how. It has to be someone who has access to your authorization for payment slips. See, someone has to have been turning in phony requisitions for payment, then picking up the money at the mailboxes and endorsing them and putting them in their own bank account." He paused. "Or else someone with access to the money is just writing checks without bothering with the requisition slips."

"Oh, no, they couldn't do that. Only Kelly has check signing authorization, and—"

She stopped, her eyes widening. "Oh, my God. That's what you're saying, isn't it? You think it's Kelly who's stealing from us!"

Bryce sighed and reached out to take her hands. "I'm sorry, Angela, but yes, she's the most likely candidate."

Angela jerked her hands out of his. "Are you insane? It couldn't be Kelly! Anyway, Tim or I have to countersign all the checks."

Bryce shook his head. "Do you honestly mean to tell me that whenever Kelly gives you checks to sign, you check out whether it's legitimate? Do you even look at the checks before you sign them?"

"No," Angela admitted. "But why couldn't it be what you said before, that someone is filling out phony authorizations, and she just writes the checks? I mean, if she has an authorization slip, she wouldn't question it."

"No. Kelly explained the system to me when I first got here. For payments as large as these, the authorization has to be approved by either you or Tim."

"Well, they could have forged our signatures!" Angela retorted. "Isn't that possible? Or maybe whoever did it gave us some story, made it seem reasonable for us to pay them."

"But you and Tim had never heard of any of these companies."

"Well, then, forgery." Angela set her jaw stubbornly. "You don't know Kelly. I do. She could not have done this to us."

"I checked the authorization slips. There are copies in the accounting office. And there's not a single authorization slip for any of these expenditures. Only Kelly wouldn't need an authorization slip. All she would have to do is add these accounts to the computer and key in the figures whenever she wanted another payment."

"No. It's impossible."

"I'm afraid it's very possible. She holds a great deal of power in your company. She could do this without being questioned. And who was to notice? Neither you nor Tim like the business side of the company. He's into computers, and you're into stories. The product was all that either of you thought about. You were careless about the rest of it. Running the office didn't interest you."

"I'll admit that. But it doesn't mean that Kelly did this. It could have been someone else. You have no proof that it was her."

"No. We'll have to leave that up to the police."

"The police!"

"Yes, of course. This is embezzlement. It's a crime. They will question Kelly and the other employees. They'll check into everyone's finances. If someone's been spending way over their income, it'll show."

"Oh, God." Angela plunged her fingers into her hair, pulling it backward. "This is a nightmare. It couldn't, it just couldn't have been Kelly. You can't turn her into the police."

"I'm not turning her in. I will simply give them the facts."

"And point out that Kelly's the obvious suspect!" Angela flared.

Bryce's mouth tightened. "For some reason, I thought you would be glad to discover where your money's been going. I would have thought you would like to know who did it and make sure that that person gets punished."

"Not if it means that Kelly gets railroaded into prison!"

"She won't be railroaded."

"She didn't do it! You don't know her like I do. She is incapable of stealing. Why, she has trouble even telling a lie. I've seen her—she gets all twitchy."

"She didn't have to lie to you to take this money."

"She's my friend. We've been friends for ten years. We go shopping together, we go to the movies." Angela stopped and grimaced. "Okay, maybe that sounds silly, but I know she wouldn't betray me. She wouldn't do anything to hurt Tim or me."

"It's easy to tell yourself that doing this sort of thing wouldn't really hurt you and Tim. Maybe the business makes a little bit less profit, but it's not like it's going to bankrupt either of you. She wouldn't envision that the trouble with the IRS might arise. I'm sure she felt that her tracks were amply covered."

"Kelly would not steal from Tim and me! The three of us are practically family."

"I have news for you. Even family members steal from each other."

"You're so cynical." Angela glared at him.

"I'm realistic." Bryce folded his arms across his chest and stared stonily back at her.

"Then give me one good reason why she would do it. She makes a good salary—a very good salary."

"But not as good as what you and Tim make. You two are the owners of the company."

"Kelly has shares in H & A."

"It's not the same. Think of it from her point of view. She started out with you in the beginning. She's always done all the financial work. Might she not start to feel resentful, to think, 'Look at all I've done for this company, yet I'm not a partner. That isn't fair. Where would they be without me?' Maybe she looks at all the things she's done and thinks she should be compensated more. Maybe she looks at what you have and feels envy. Sure, she's making great money for someone her age, with her credentials. Yes, you've given her a lot. But that isn't necessarily enough for some people. Sometimes they're eaten up with jealousy and resentment. If she were, she might very well decide to rectify what she perceives as an injustice."

Angela stared at him in horror. "No! Kelly's not like that at all. I remember her telling me once that she's glad that she doesn't have the weight of the company on her back, that she wouldn't like to have the responsibility. Besides, she knows that it's Tim's and my work that *is* the business."

"People don't always tell the truth." He pointed this out reasonably.

"Well, they don't always lie, either!" Angela snapped back. "Why are you so determined to make Kelly the villain?"

"I'm not. I'm just looking at the facts, and they all point to—"

"Forget your damn facts!" Angela blazed. "I *know* Kelly, and I know she could not have done it!"

Bryce groaned. "You're being irrational."

"And you're being cold and inhuman!"

"I'm being logical. Dammit, Angela, you're letting your emotions carry you away. You have no basis for believing that Kelly didn't do it."

"I do have a basis for it! It's something you wouldn't understand. My basis is ten years of being around her, of knowing her, of seeing her do things, hearing what she says. Simply because I pay attention to my emotions doesn't mean I'm an idiot. It means that I notice the intangibles. I process those other things that are just as important, if not more important, than the black-and-white facts! I've always acted on my gut instinct in my business, and it's proven very successful."

"This isn't the same. Gut instincts may be fine in judging what games people are going to like or dislike. But they don't stand up against factual proof. Why are you being so damn pigheaded about this?"

"I'm not. I simply have different values than you." Angela looked at him coldly. "I believe in things like trust and friendship. I value *feelings*. Obviously you don't."

"Kelly has betrayed your friendship and trust. You don't owe her any loyalty. You're just being naive."

"That's better than having no heart!"

"Don't be a fool," he began roughly, reaching out to take her arm.

She jerked away from him. "No! Don't touch me. I don't know how I could have ever fallen in love with you! You're exactly what I thought you were to begin with—an inhuman machine, cold and logical, incapable of understanding anything but numbers. You don't know how to feel. You couldn't fall in love because it's not written down in a column of numbers!"

Angela whirled and stormed out of the living room, slamming the front door after her for good measure. Bryce, left standing behind her, let out a string of curses and slammed his hand against the wall.

Damn that woman! She was so pigheaded and irrational, so determined not to listen to reason!

He was tempted to get back into his car and drive back to Charlotte. *Let her continue to be sucked dry by her supposed friend; let her try out her "gut instinct" and "feelings" theory on the IRS.*

But he knew he could not do that. *It would be like...like abandoning the woman he loved.* Bryce sat down abruptly on the couch; he felt for a moment strangely unsteady. Angela was infuriating; she was far too emotional, too impulsive. Not at all the sort of woman for him. He had told himself so a million times. But now he admitted that she was the only woman he wanted. However infuriating and emotional and impulsive she was, she was also the warmth and love he had been searching for all his life. He thought of what she had said, that she didn't know how she could have fallen in love with him, and he smiled. *She loved him, too.* It was absurd and irrational, but it was true, and Bryce knew that he would not have it any other way.

He sighed and leaned back, gazing up at the ceiling. He decided he would wait until she returned, and then— He paused, frowning. *Where had she gone, anyway?* He hadn't heard her knock on the condo next door, so she hadn't gone there to unload her troubles on her friends. Perhaps she had gone for a walk to cool off. Or maybe a ride—he thought he had heard a car start a few moments after she left.

Suddenly Bryce sat bolt upright on the couch as a new thought seized him. He knew where she had gone. She would have wanted to tell Kelly what he had said; she would be sure, so blastedly, trustingly *sure* that Kelly would be able to prove she had not done it. A chill ran through Bryce. White-collar criminals were rarely dangerous, but one never knew what any person might do if she felt cornered and scared. If Kelly realized that Angela was on to her, it was possible that she would try to shut her up, keep her from going to the police. She might in a moment of anger or fear lash out at Angela, especially if the reason for her theft was, as Bryce had surmised, years of built-up envy and resentment.

He jumped to his feet and started toward the front door, then remembered belatedly that he had no idea where Kelly lived. He could go down to the office and find the address, of course, but that would eat up more valuable time—and Angela already had quite a head start on him.

Bryce hurried to the telephone. There was a button on the memory phone with the word "Tim" beside it, and he punched it. A child's voice answered, then left to find its father, and Bryce waited, his fingers drumming against the wall impatiently. When Tim's good-humored voice came on the line, Bryce launched into a quick summary of what he had found out, ending with a demand for Kelly's address.

There was a long moment of stunned silence on the other end of the line. Finally Tim said, "What? I can't believe it."

"That doesn't matter right now. Just give me Kelly's address. Angela's gone over there, I'm sure, and I don't know what might happen."

"Yeah. Sure." His voice still dazed with shock, Tim gave him the address of Kelly's home and directions on how to get there.

Bryce slammed down the phone and hurried out the front door.

Twelve

Angela pulled into the single driveway of Kelly's house and jumped out, not bothering to lock the car. Kelly's house was a quaint little cottage in an older neighborhood, which she had bought three years ago and spent all her spare time renovating. It was shaded by huge trees, from one of which an old-fashioned swing hung. Angela had sat there with Kelly many times on a spring or summer evening.

She pelted up the stairs to rap furiously at Kelly's door.

"Okay, okay," she heard Kelly's voice on the other side of the door, and an instant later, it swung open. Kelly's eyebrows went up. "What in the world are you pounding like that for?" She peered at Angela more closely, and her blue eyes registered alarm. "Angela? What's the matter?"

"Bryce thinks you did it." Angela swept past Kelly into the small living room and began to pace across its pine-floored length.

"Bryce thinks I did what?" Kelly asked in confusion, following her.

"He thinks you've been embezzling from us. He thinks that's why our profits are down."

Kelly stared at her. "Embezzling?" she repeated blankly.

"Yes, embezzling," Angela repeated impatiently. "We have to figure out how to prove that you didn't do it. He's going to put the police on it, and they'll probably jump to the obvious conclusion like Bryce did. Since you're the one who's in charge of the books, you must be the one who did it."

"Wait. Stop. You left me way behind. Sit down, and tell me what you're talking about."

Angela drew a calming breath and did as Kelly suggested. As quickly and coherently as she could, she outlined what Bryce had told her about the payments made to apparently fictitious companies over the course of the year.

"No wonder Bryce was bustling around so today. I thought something must be going on. But the way he kept phoning his office, I figured it was something there, something they were working on."

"Kelly!" Angela snapped. "Would you concentrate on how to prove you didn't do it? You could be in real trouble here."

Kelly nodded and knotted her brow in a frown. "Brachen? F & F? I don't remember anything about them. What was the other one?"

"I'm not sure. Something in California. Oh, uh, ALM. ALF, something like that."

"Angie, none of this is ringing a bell with me."

"Of course not. Why would you notice a few payments to two or three companies? They weren't regular things. Although they were large—$20,000, $10,000."

"Actually, I don't usually do the books. Connie runs the spreadsheets."

"Could she have been doing it?"

"Embezzling? Oh, no! That is, well, I don't think so. I can't imagine it. I mean, I guess she could have forged our signatures, but—no, I just can't see it. Somebody must have put in requisition slips for them." She paused, frowning with thought. "Wait a minute, I do have a vague memory of one of them. That Brachen thing. I'm sure I would have checked it against the requisition slips."

"That's one of the problems. Bryce said he checked in the office, and there were no requisition slips for any of them."

"He must have looked in the wrong place," Kelly insisted. She jumped to her feet. "Come on. Let's go down to the office. I'm sure I'll be able to find them."

Bryce couldn't be right, Angela thought, as she followed Kelly out to the car. Kelly did not look in the slightest guilty. She had obviously been as stunned and surprised as Angela had been when Bryce told her. Kelly simply could not be that good an actress. Hope began to rise in Angela as she slid in behind the steering wheel and turned on the engine. *When they got to the office, Kelly would be able to find the requisition slips, and somehow from that they would be able to find out who the real embezzler was.*

When they reached the office, Angela pulled into the empty graveled area behind the house and parked.

The house was dark; all the other employees had obviously left. Angela and Kelly went in the back door, entering through the kitchen of the old house, and walked through the wide corridor to the door of the accounting department.

Kelly opened it with a key and, flipping on a switch, walked straight across the room to a filing cabinet. She opened it with another, smaller, key and pulled out the middle drawer. She took out a thick folder of computer paper and laid it on a table, then began to search through it.

"Okay, here's one. F & F, May 16. The requisition slips are filed by date." She went over to a counter, where a small file sat and pulled out its drawer, then began to flip through its contents until she found the tab she wanted. She riffled through it quickly, then stopped.

"That's weird. There's nothing here for it." She pulled a wad of pink slips out and laid them down on the counter and went through them again, more slowly. Finally she sighed and looked up worriedly at Angela. "It's not here."

"Try another one."

"Okay." She returned to the large folder and began to search again. After a while she found another date and returned to the requisition file. She sorted through it, then turned to Angela, lines deepening in her forehead. "It's not here, either."

"Oh, God." Angela plopped down despondently in one of the desk chairs. "What are we going to do? Is there anyplace else they could be?"

"Just those particular requisition slips? Not likely." Kelly chewed her lower lip.

"Well, look, is there another copy of the payment orders?"

Kelly brightened. "Sure! Why didn't I think of that? It's a carbon form. One copy of it goes to accounting, and the other goes into a file that the person who orders it keeps!" Her eyes widened. "That would pretty much tell us who it was, wouldn't it? The person who put in the request for the payment."

"Yeah. The only problem is we have to know who did it before we can find the other copy."

Kelly nodded. "Yes. And he isn't likely to have kept them, either. That must be why these are missing— they've removed them so the payment can't be traced back to them."

"You're right." Angela rested her elbow on the desk in front of her and propped her chin on her hand, thinking.

"Well, look," Kelly began, trying to be cheerful. "The police won't be able to prove I did it. All they'll have is suspicion. I mean, they won't find any extravagant spending on my part or any deposits in my bank account or anything."

Angela's hopes rose, but then she shook her head firmly, rising from her chair. "No. We have to find out who it is. Otherwise, this suspicion will hang over you all your life, even if the police can't prove that you did it. You sit here and think about those accounts. Try to remember if anyone ever mentioned them to you. I'll go make us some tea. Then we'll search the payment order files in everyone's office, if we have to."

"Okay." Kelly walked over to one of the computer terminals and sat down, beginning to boot up the machine. "Let me look at the company's files. Maybe that will jog my memory. What were their names, besides Brachen?''

''ALM and F & F Graphics.''

''You know, that ALM one sounds vaguely familiar.'' Her voice drifted off as she began to type.

Angela left Kelly in front of the computer screen and walked back through the hall into the kitchen. She filled two cups with water and put them into the microwave, then pulled out two bags of herbal tea and stood waiting for the microwave to beep.

A loud click out in the hall startled Angela from her reverie. It was followed by the sound of the front door opening and closing. Curious, Angela walked to the doorway to look out in the hall.

''Tim!''

Her partner was standing at the foot of the stairs, two empty boxes in his hands. He jumped at the sound of her voice and whirled around.

''Angela!'' He looked surprised. ''I didn't see your car out front.''

''We parked in the back. This is great. I'm glad you're here. You can help us.'' She glanced down at the boxes in his hands. ''What are you doing?''

''What? Oh.'' Tim looked down blankly at the boxes in his hands. ''I was... I came up here to get some things out of my office. Some plants. They're dying, and I figured Melanie might be able to revive them. How about you? What are you doing up here?''

''Kelly and I are looking for some payment orders.''

''Payment orders?''

''Yeah. Oh, Tim, it's such a mess. Bryce thinks Kelly has been stealing from us, and we can't find the payment orders for the checks that accounting wrote.

But you can help us. You can probably figure out a way from the computer to find out who put in the orders."

"I don't know. I'll try. Let me go up and take those things out to my car, and I'll take a look, okay?"

"Okay."

He started toward the stairs, and Angela turned to go back into the kitchen, when there came a shout from the accounting office, "Angela!"

Kelly came hurrying down the stairs, looking over the railing at Angela. Her face glowed with excitement. "I remembered! I could remember making a note about it sometime ago, so I went up to my office and looked back through my calendar. And there it was. ALM—Tim. I talked to Tim about it."

She stopped abruptly, and all the color drained from her face. "Oh, my God."

"What? Kelly!" Angela took an anxious step toward her, but a strangled noise from the bottom of the stairs stopped her.

Kelly turned her head and looked at the foot of the stairs. For the first time she saw Tim and, if possible, she turned even paler. "Oh, Tim . . . no!"

Angela froze, staring at Tim. He stood stock-still, the cardboard boxes dangling foolishly from his hands. His face was pale, and sweat dotted his forehead and upper lip. His brown eyes were wide and frightened and filled with guilt.

"Tim?" Angela squeaked. She felt suddenly sick to her stomach, and tears flooded her eyes.

Kelly said tonelessly, "I remember I called him and asked him what it was, who it had come from because it was his name on the authorization, but there was no name on the top line—who was requesting the payment, you know. He said he was the one who had requested it, that ALM was a company that was working on some kind of new chip that would really speed up our games. And I just filled in his name on the line and forgot about it. It didn't seem very important at the time.''

With a curse, Tim turned away, flinging the cardboard boxes against the door. He turned toward Angela and Kelly, frustration and despair in every line of his face. For the first time since she had known him, Angela felt a tiny thrill of fear run down her spine. She thought suddenly about the fact that she and Kelly were alone with Tim in the office—and that he would be ruined when they told what they knew.

She must have taken an involuntary step backward, because Tim's eyes widened and hurt swept over his features. "Do you think I'm going to hurt you? Angela! I would never do anything like that. You know me.''

"I don't know," she replied tearfully. "All of a sudden, I don't know you at all anymore.''

He spread out his hands in a supplicating gesture. "I'm sorry. I never meant for anyone to get hurt by this. I thought I could do it and no one would ever notice. I sure never dreamed it would set the IRS on us or bring that damn bloodhound Richards down here. I didn't mean to make it look like Kelly had done it. Please, you have to believe me. I would never intentionally hurt you or Kelly.''

"But why, Tim? Why would you do it?" Kelly asked. "You own half the company. You get half the profits.''

"A lot of that we put back into the company. More than that, taxes wipe out a big chunk of it. This was income that wasn't reported to the IRS. I didn't have to pay any taxes on it." He gave them a wry grin. "You think H & A Enterprises was in trouble with the IRS, wait until you see what they do to *me* now."

He groaned and sank onto the bottom step, bracing his head on his hands. "I lost a lot of money in real estate investments a few years ago. I was paying heavy interest on the pieces of land, and I couldn't sell them. I was in a mess. It was eating up all our savings and our other investments. But I couldn't declare bankruptcy. And I couldn't watch Melanie and the kids having to do without the things they were accustomed to. I managed to sell some of the property and stay afloat, but about two years ago, I was at the end of my rope. Then I came up with this idea. I'd borrow it from the company. I always meant to return it! But once I'd started...I don't know, it was too handy. And I loved giving Melanie and the kids things. You know how I am with money—it just melts away. I couldn't— oh, hell, I couldn't admit to anybody what a failure I'd been, how stupidly I'd acted. I kept thinking, well, the market's coming back now. In a year or two, I'll be able to get all these things off my hands, and I'll pay the company back then."

"How? How could you possibly stick back in several hundred thousand dollars without anybody noticing?"

"I figured I'd come up with something. After all, I had managed to get it out." Tim grinned at Angela sheepishly. "You know how I am."

Angela groaned. "Oh, Tim..." She had always known of his ostrich tendencies, his way of hoping that things would go away or work themselves out if he simply ignored them. Usually it was a fairly harmless personality quirk. This time it had led him into severe trouble.

"Maybe . . . maybe we could still think of some way to work it out," Tim began, brightening a little. "If I sold some stuff and replaced the money . . ."

"That's a good place to start," said a male voice behind them, and they all started in surprise and turned to look back at the kitchen door. Bryce stood in the doorway, arms folded, leaning against the doorjamb.

"Bryce! What are you doing here?"

"I got worried about you after you left. I figured you went to tell Kelly about what I'd told you, and I was afraid of what might happen to you. I followed you over there, and when you two weren't there, I figured you would be at the office, so I drove here. Unfortunately I had fingered the wrong villain." Bryce looked at Angela, and a faint smile touched his lips. "I was too involved with my client. I didn't look as objectively as I should have into the case. I started with the given that the owners weren't guilty of fraud because I was in love with one of them."

Tears sprang into Angela's eyes again, but she smiled tenderly at Bryce while the tears rolled down her cheeks. Bryce walked over to her and wiped her tears away with his hand, then kissed her lightly on the forehead.

"Anyway, I had called Tim to get Kelly's address and tell him the situation. I expected him to meet me at Kelly's. Instead he must have seized the opportunity to come over here and get rid of some incriminating evidence."

They both turned to look back at Tim.

He sighed wearily. "No, I knew it was up when you told me you thought Kelly did it. I had gotten rid of the payment orders in accounting when you said you were looking into those companies. But that didn't stop you—it just incriminated Kelly. I knew once the three of you started talking, it wouldn't be long before you figured out that it was really me. I came over here to get some of my things, then I was going to get out of the country."

"Tim!" Angela exclaimed, her face falling into lines of disillusion. "You mean you were going to leave Melanie and the kids here to face it alone? And what if Kelly hadn't remembered that you authorized it? Or nobody would believe her?"

"Come on, Ange, that wouldn't happen. As soon as I disappeared, everybody would know it was me. Besides, I was going to mail a letter confessing when I got on the plane. And Melanie and the kids will be better off without me. If I wasn't here, they wouldn't have to face all that trial and everything. The publicity would have blown over in a few days, and they could have gone back to normal."

"With the IRS impounding your assets?" Bryce said sarcastically. "I don't think so. You're obviously into fantasy big time. But for once, Tim, you're going to have to face the music. The only way you can help your family or H & A Enterprises is to stay right here, get a good lawyer and see what kind of deal you can work out with the government."

Bryce gave him a smile that was more a baring of teeth and added, "Anyway, I'm here to see that that's what you do whether you want to or not. It'll mean the least publicity and hurt for Angela, too."

He walked across the hallway and grasped Tim firmly by the arm. Hauling him to his feet, he said, "Come on, let's call your tax attorney and see if he knows any good *criminal* lawyers."

Angela turned and shot an anguished glance across the hall at Kelly. Kelly shook her head. She looked as stunned and disbelieving as Angela felt. *How could she have been so deceived by Tim?* Angela had never before felt this kind of hurt and betrayal.

She turned on her heel and walked back through the kitchen, grabbing her car keys from the table where she had dropped them when they came in. She hurried down the back steps and across the graveled lot to her car. Tears were forming in her eyes, blurring her vision. Quickly she got in and turned on the engine, blinking the tears away. Then she backed out of the driveway and into the street. She knew that Bryce would wonder where she was. He probably had wanted her to stay there to help the police with the investigation.

But she could not bear to be around when the police came. Tim had been her good friend and business partner for eight years. They had laughed together, dreamed together, sweated out those first few months of their business together. He was more like a brother than a friend. It tore at her insides to think of him being handcuffed and hauled off to jail, subjected to the trial and prison. *And poor Melanie!* Sobs welled up in Angela's throat at the thought of Tim's wife. It would be a nightmare for her and the children.

Yet at the same time that she felt almost sick with sorrow for Tim and his family, she also was bitterly hurt and disillusioned. Tim had betrayed her and their business. He had cheated her, lied to her, broken the bond of friendship that she had thought was so firm. It left her empty and angry and shocked.

At first Angela drove aimlessly through the streets of Raleigh, but soon, without her even being aware of it, she was on the highway going north toward Lake Gaston. It was where she always went when she was in need of peace and healing. She drove, wiping away the tears that streamed silently down her face, her mind a jumble of thoughts and emotions.

When she finally reached the lake, she sat down in her favorite chair and gave way completely to her tears. Sometime later, she got up and washed her face, grimacing a little at her blotchy face in the mirror, then made a cup of coffee and went out onto the deck to watch the sun sinking in the west. It was soothing to sit there, sipping the hot liquid and watching the sky blaze with gold and red, then gradually settle into monochrome.

Finally, when the spring air grew too cool, she went back inside and made a fire to take away the chill of the evening. But it wasn't enough to take away the chill inside her. The lake was not doing its usual job of removing her problems. There was an aching emptiness inside her. She realized that she wished Bryce were there. Nothing would seem as bad with his arms around her.

Angela dozed on the couch, mesmerized by the flames. She was awakened an hour later by the bright lights of a car flashing through the window. She sat up in confusion; it took a moment to remember where she was and what had led her to be there.

Outside the car lights went off and the engine died. A moment later, there was a knock on the door. Angela thought of Bryce, and she jumped up eagerly and hurried toward the door. Peeping out the side window, she saw that it was indeed Bryce, and she swung open the door with a cry of delight.

"Bryce!" She flung herself against him.

He looked weary in the porch light, but he smiled at her greeting and wrapped his arms around her tightly.

"Hello, sweetheart. How are you?"

"I'm okay." She kissed him and stepped back, taking his hand and leading him inside. Everything seemed much more cheerful now that he was here with her. "How did you know I was out here?"

He shrugged. "I figured this would be where you'd go when you were upset."

"You're right. I had a good cry."

"Did it help?"

"I don't know. I guess so." Angela sighed. "Oh, Bryce, I still can't believe that it's true."

"It's true, all right," Bryce replied grimly.

They walked over to the couch and settled down upon it, his arm looped around her shoulders.

"I'm sorry I left. I just couldn't stand to stay there and see it."

"I know. It was fine. Kelly went home, too. Tim was very cooperative."

"What's going to happen to him?"

"I don't know. They usually don't go as hard on white-collar crimes, and it's his first offense. Plus, he turned himself in, and he had a good lawyer with him. My guess is he'll pay the money back to the company and plea-bargain down to a fine and a little time in jail, maybe even probation."

"But where will he get the money? You heard him, he needed it. I'm sure he's spent it already."

"He has plenty of assets. That house, primarily—an estate like that'll bring plenty. And cars, etc."

"Poor Tim. Poor Melanie."

"Don't feel too sorry for him. He put you and Kelly and your company through a lot of hell."

"I know." Angela sighed. "Well, that'll mean we can pay the taxes we owe. They won't prosecute us, will they, since Tim was defrauding the company? I mean, we didn't realize those charges weren't legitimate expenses."

"I don't imagine so. Payment, plus late fees and interest will probably satisfy the bloodsuckers."

Angela hesitated, then said, "I'm sorry for those things I said to you earlier today."

A corner of his mouth lifted. "I've heard them before."

"Maybe. But I shouldn't have said them. And you were right—I was naive and stupid."

"No. Maybe you shouldn't have trusted Tim so easily, but you had every reason to. And you were absolutely right about Kelly. I was wrong. She hadn't done anything criminal, and you stuck by her. You believed in her. Your loyalty and faith are wonderful qualities. I shouldn't have said what I did. And I didn't mean it. I was angry." He paused, then said quietly, "You didn't believe me, and that hurt. I felt as if you were choosing your friend over me."

"No! I would never do that. I just thought you were wrong. It didn't mean anything about who I love the most. I mean, I love Kelly and Tim...we've been friends for years. But it doesn't compare to how I feel about you."

Bryce turned sideways so that he could look into her face. "Do you really mean that? You haven't told me."

Angela gave him a wry smile. "I didn't think you'd want to hear it. I mean, I'm romantic and emotional, you're practical and logical. I know that our being together made you uneasy. Just because I felt certain of my feelings didn't mean that you did. I was afraid you'd run for the hills if I dumped that load on you."

"Oh, Angela." He took a strand of her hair and began to wind it around his finger. The look on his face made the blood begin to pulse faster in Angela's veins. "I love you. I've just been too hardheaded and scared to admit it. I've gotten through life by telling myself I didn't need emotions...logic was everything. I didn't need love. I didn't need a family. But you made me see the truth. I need love. I need you...desperately. When I realized you must have gone to confront Kelly and I thought that she might hurt you, it scared me to death. I knew how empty life would be without you. And I wondered why in the world I had fought so hard to keep you out of my life."

"'Cause you're hardheaded," Angela told him with a chuckle, taking his hand and raising it to her lips. She kissed his palm and rubbed her cheek sensuously against it. "But I love you anyway."

"I may be hardheaded," Bryce said, taking her by the shoulders and pulling her onto his lap, "but I'm not a fool." He kissed her lingeringly, then asked, "Angela, will you marry me?"

Angela looked up at him, flushed and a trifle dazed, her lips soft and moist from his kiss. "What? Are you serious?"

"Of course I'm serious. Don't you remember? I'm the man with no sense of humor."

She smiled. "Of course. How could I forget?"

"Well? Do you think you could live with a serious, practical, logical old stick-in-the-mud?"

"Yes! Oh, yes, I could live with one, as long as it's you." Angela threw her arms around his neck and kissed him all over his face, punctuating each kiss with a decisive, "Yes."

She drew back suddenly, frowning a little. "But where are we going to live? Your business is in Charlotte, and mine's here, and how—"

"Don't worry, we'll work it out." He grinned and pulled her back into his arms. "Don't be so damn practical."

Angela chuckled, melting into his arms. "If you insist."

*   *   *   *   *

COMING NEXT MONTH

It's Silhouette Desire's 1000th birthday! Join us for a spectacular three-month celebration, starring your favorite authors and the hottest heroes of the decade!

#991 SADDLE UP—Mary Lynn Baxter

One night with Bridget Martin had cost April's *Man of the Month*, single dad Jeremiah Davis, his bachelorhood! But would his new bride be the perfect mom for his little girl?

#992 THE GROOM, I PRESUME?—Annette Broadrick

Daughters of Texas

Maribeth O'Brien was everything Chris Cochran wanted in a woman. So when she was left at the altar by her delinquent groom, Chris stepped in and said, "I do"!

#993 FATHER OF THE BRAT—Elizabeth Bevarly

From Here to Paternity

Maddy Garrett had never liked arrogant Carver Venner. But now he needed her help—and Maddy couldn't resist his adorable daughter...or the sexy single dad!

#994 A STRANGER IN TEXAS—Lass Small

One passionate encounter with a handsome stranger had left Jessica Channing one very pregnant woman. Now the mysterious man was back, determined to discover Jessica's secret!

#995 FORGOTTEN VOWS—Modean Moon

The Wedding Night

Although Edward Carlton claimed his lovely bride had left him on their wedding night, Jennie didn't remember her husband. But she'd do anything to discover the truth about her past—and her marriage....

#996 TWO WEDDINGS AND A BRIDE—Anne Eames

Debut Author

Brand-new bride Catherine Mason was furious when she caught her groom kissing her bridesmaid! So she went on her honeymoon with handsome Jake Alley—and hoped another wedding would soon be on the way....

MILLION DOLLAR SWEEPSTAKES

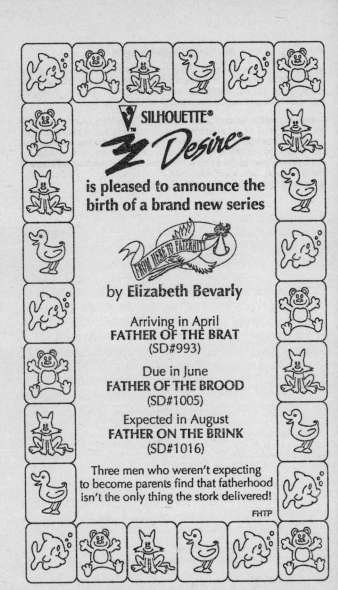

PROTECTORS

by Beverly Barton

Trained to protect, ready to lay their lives on the line, but unprepared for the power of love.

Award-winning author Beverly Barton brings you
Ashe McLaughlin, Sam Dundee and J. T. Blackwood...
three rugged, sexy ex-government agents—each with a
special woman to protect.

J.T. Blackwood is six feet four inches of whipcord-lean man.
And in April, in BLACKWOOD'S WOMAN (IM #707), the
former secret service agent returns to his New Mexico ranch
for a well-deserved vacation, and finds his most dangerous
assignment yet—Joanna Beaumont. The terror Joanna fled
from five years ago has suddenly found her. Now only J.T.
stands between his beautiful tenant's deadly past and her
future...a future he is determined to share with her.

And if you missed Books 1 and 2 of THE PROTECTORS, you can still get your copies
now. To order Ashe McLaughlin's story, DEFENDING HIS OWN, IM #670, or Sam
Dundee's story, GUARDING JEANNIE, IM #688, please send your name, address, zip
or postal code, along with a check or money order (please do not send cash) for
$3.75 for each book ordered ($4.25 in Canada), plus 75¢ postage and handling ($1.00
in Canada), payable to Silhouette Books, to:

In the U.S.	In Canada
Silhouette Books	Silhouette Books
3010 Walden Ave.	P. O. Box 636
P. O. Box 9077	Fort Erie, Ontario
Buffalo, NY 14269-9077	L2A 5X3

Please specify book title(s) with your order.
Canadian residents add applicable federal and provincial taxes.

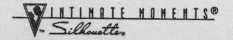

INTIMATE MOMENTS®
Silhouette®

BBPROT3

Witness what happens when a devil falls
in love with an angel

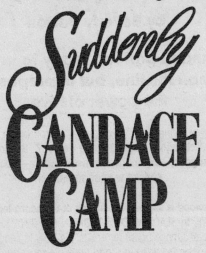

Suddenly

CANDACE
CAMP

Simon "Devil" Dure needs a wife, and Charity Emerson is
sure she can meet his expectations…and then some.

Charity is right, and the Devil is finally seduced by her
crazy schemes, her warm laughter, her loving heart. There
is no warning, however, of the dangerous trap that lies
ahead, or of the vicious act of murder that will put their
courage—and their love—to the ultimate test.

Available at your favorite retail outlet in February.

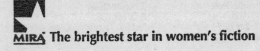

As seen on TV!
Free Gift Offer

With a Free Gift proof-of-purchase from any Silhouette® book,
you can receive a beautiful cubic zirconia pendant.

This gorgeous marquise-shaped stone is a genuine cubic
zirconia—accented by an 18" gold tone necklace.

(Approximate retail value $19.95)

Send for yours today...
compliments of **Silhouette®**

To receive your free gift, a cubic zirconia pendant, send us one original proof-of-purchase, photocopies not accepted, from the back of any Silhouette Romance™, Silhouette Desire®, Silhouette Special Edition®, Silhouette Intimate Moments® or Silhouette Shadows™ title available in February, March or April at your favorite retail outlet, together with the Free Gift Certificate, plus a check or money order for $1.75 U.S./$2.25 CAN. (do not send cash) to cover postage and handling, payable to Silhouette Free Gift Offer. We will send you the specified gift. Allow 6 to 8 weeks for delivery. Offer good until April 30, 1996 or while quantities last. Offer valid in the U.S. and Canada only.

Free Gift Certificate

Name: _____

Address: _____

City: _____ State/Province: _____ Zip/Postal Code: _____

Mail this certificate, one proof-of-purchase and a check or money order for postage and handling to: SILHOUETTE FREE GIFT OFFER 1996. In the U.S.: 3010 Walden Avenue, P.O. Box 9057, Buffalo NY 14269-9057. In Canada: P.O. Box 622, Fort Erie,

---

FREE GIFT OFFER   079-KBZ-R
ONE PROOF-OF-PURCHASE
To collect your fabulous FREE GIFT, a cubic zirconia pendant, you must include this
original proof-of-purchase for each gift with the properly completed Free Gift Certificate.

079-KBZ-R

You're About to Become a *Privileged Woman*

Reap the rewards of fabulous free gifts and benefits with proofs-of-purchase from Silhouette and Harlequin books

Pages & Privileges™

It's our way of thanking you for buying our books at your favorite retail stores.

**Harlequin and Silhouette—
the most privileged readers in the world!**

For more information about Harlequin and Silhouette's PAGES & PRIVILEGES program call the Pages & Privileges Benefits Desk: 1-503-794-2499

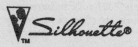